SIMPLY MARVELOUS

"You either want to be with me or you don't. Make up your mind one way or the other."

Her voice and face held a look of warning. "Don't make me choose."

He'd never been this angry with her before. Ever. "What in the world are you talking about, Daisy? Choose? Choose what? We're a couple, aren't we?"

Daisy's pulse felt arrested. Time stopped. This was a turning point for them—explosive, life-altering, imperative. She said softly, "Yes." Her paranoia about the future was one thing, but her love for Kenneth was clear in her mind.

"Then there is no choice," he stated flatly. "It's a continuation. You can't have a rose without the basics—sun, soil, and water. You can't have a relationship without the basics either—as in trust, faith, and fidelity. I believe in you as my lover and as my friend. If that's not enough for you, nothing will ever be and we might as well end this thing now because a thing is all it is."

SIMPLY MARVELOUS

Shelby Lewis

BET Publications LLC

ARABESQUE BOOKS are published by

BET Publications, LLC
c/o BET BOOKS
One BET Plaza
1900 W Place NE
Washington, DC 20018-1211

ISBN 0- 7394- 2423- 8

Printed in the United States of America

Marvin,

You were the first to say, "Welcome."
I still see that boy and his smile in the man you are today.
In dreams, Marvin, everything is possible.
Live your dreams.

Sis

AUTHOR'S NOTE

What is a flower show?

A flower show is an event that celebrates the beauty of flowers grown in private or commercial gardens for public exhibition. It is a place where ordinary gardeners and experts are free to share ideas on topics ranging from soil and water management to pest control and hybridization. It is a place where unique discoveries in the flower growing arena and exceptional plant beauty are fairly judged and honored. But sometimes, as is the case with this story, the competitive spirit can get out of control . . . and even be deadly.

One

Saturday afternoon,
first week of June

When Kenneth Gunn stepped off the airplane, he had no idea he was stepping into a drama-filled week. A private detective in Wichita, Kansas, he'd made plans for a romantic visit with his girlfriend, Daisy Rogers, a retail nursery and garden shop owner in Guthrie, Oklahoma. The only strain in their relationship was the long traveling distance between them. It meant they couldn't see each other every day the way they wanted to, which made their time together that much sweeter.

On this occasion, Kenneth was flying in from a business trip in Dallas where he'd just finished solving a missing persons case, one that had ended on a positive note; he'd been able to reunite a runaway teen with his family. Kenneth looked forward to some quality downtime with Daisy, his way of regrouping between cases.

In order to get to Guthrie, he'd flown from Dallas on a commuter airplane to the Will Rogers Airport in Oklahoma City. From this point, he needed a car to get from Oklahoma City to Guthrie, which he preferred so that he'd have his own wheels during his brief holiday. However, on this trip, Daisy had opted to pick him up in her full-size Chevy truck. Kenneth had never dated a woman who owned a truck before, and he couldn't imagine Daisy driving anything different.

Daisy. The excitement of seeing her again made Kenneth forget that the small airplane had been too hot and that a seven-month-old baby girl aboard had cried the whole way. He'd found himself eyeing the small brown baby and wondering if he'd ever have one of his own. If he did, he'd want a girl, one who looked just like Daisy.

Daisy. Kenneth wondered if she'd pick him up wearing a next-to-nothing dress or her usual jeans, T-shirt, and green rubber gardening clogs. She looked good in everything or nothing at all, his favorite way to see her whenever they were alone together. Whatever she wore, she was never self-conscious, and he liked the way she was so relaxed with herself. She was pretty without primping and he liked this, too.

Dressed all in black, Kenneth strode through the quiet, makeshift tunnel from the plane to the lobby and straight into Daisy's arms. She felt soft and warm and cuddly. He was hard in an instant. "Baby," he said low in her ear, "it's been six weeks too long."

They had talked on the phone as often as

they could, but Kenneth's schedule wasn't predictable and they often missed each other, an absence they tried to remedy by talking for hours at a stretch, like teenagers in love, oblivious to the passage of time, so that hours seemed like minutes, and days were like hours.

Kenneth knew that this visit to see Daisy would feel shorter than a full seven days. Though intense, his visits seldom lasted long enough for him to feel restless for his normal routine in Wichita. He never felt as good upon leaving her home in Guthrie as he did upon arriving. Once he left, he was very conscious of time.

Hours felt like days and days were months that stretched forever until the next moment they could be together again. Without Daisy, Kenneth felt lonely. He hated feeling lonely, and for a brief moment, his dark eyes reflected that unhappy thought.

Daisy saw the moment and responded to it playfully. She placed a chaste kiss on his lips, but the look in her eyes told him a different, quite provocative story, one that revealed all the subtle details of her desires.

She, too, had been lonely, a woman keenly aware of the late hours of night when the only thing warm to hold on to tight was the pillow beside her in a bed so big, it dominated the bedroom they would soon share together.

Not a woman who restrained her feelings, Daisy's eyes stripped him stark naked in two seconds flat. Her body radiated with anticipation.

She said, "Let's skip dinner." She was a tease who knew how to please.

Kenneth's excitement jumped up a notch. He forced himself to walk and not run to her waiting vehicle. He was too old and too dignified to show the casual onlookers around them in the airport how very hot and horny he was at just the sight of the woman who refused to wear his engagement ring. He chose to grin like a fool instead, a reflection of the jittery feeling in the pit of his stomach, a feeling that reminded him he'd missed breakfast that morning in his haste to make it to the airport on time to catch his flight from Dallas.

All negativity was suspended whenever Kenneth came together with Daisy, suspended in the comfortable way that happens between people who truly enjoy each other's company and rarely run out of words to say. He spoke without thinking first, a rare treat in his line of work. On this day, at this time, all his emotions were unguarded, his happiness as open and kind as the woman whose spirit lifted his soul. "Good thing you're closed tomorrow," he said.

Daisy gave his arm a playful squeeze. His skin felt tight, the muscles rippling beneath her fingers. *Ooh,* she thought. *Ooh.* Instead of telling him flat out what she was thinking, she said a little breathlessly, "Why?"

He laughed as if the sun was shining straight into his heart, a light that was bold and bright and beautiful. Being with Daisy made him feel as if he was breathing cool mountain air. His words came out in a low growl. "We're gonna be up all night."

She leered at him. "Promise?"

"Promise."

Her laugh, delicious and sexy, sent ripples of desire along the insides of his heavy thighs. "You make me forget it's storming outside," he said.

"Oh, yeah?" she quizzed, her silky lashes fluttering ridiculously. She felt as if her very skin was energized by Kenneth's presence.

"Yeah," he said. "I was probably the one person on the plane only half-distracted by the air turbulence we had just before landing. If my flight had been later, I probably would have been delayed. Like I said, six weeks is too long between visits. I felt every second."

She spiked her voice with a come-hither note. "More reason to play hide-and-seek under the covers."

He threw an arm around her and squeezed gently. In his mind, he pictured the ebony-colored mole beneath the palm he now used to cup her shoulder bone. She had several lovely flat moles scattered over her body, but this particular mole was his favorite.

It was his spot because when he played connect the dots with his kisses, he started with the mole on her right shoulder and worked his way to the mole on her left ankle. He said, "I love the way you speak your mind."

She squeezed him back. "I love you, too, but

it's not your mind I'm thinking about right now."

He laughed with gusto. "Same here. It's why I packed only the bag I'm holding." He lifted the leather duffel in order to show her.

"No need to stop at baggage claim?"

"Nope."

Smiling, she pulled him down so she could whisper in his ear, "I like it when you talk dirty."

He dropped his hand from her shoulder in order to lock their fingers together. Her hand felt strong and soft at the same time. "Baby, you ain't heard nothin' yet."

With his bag in the rear seat of Daisy's extended cab truck, freshly detailed by Brett's Auto Detailing in Guthrie, Kenneth was glad she tossed him the keys so he could drive. Driving would keep his hands and his mind occupied during the forty-minute commute from the City to Daisy's home in Guthrie, the quaint Victorian-style town that suited her personality so perfectly.

Guthrie suited Daisy because, like her, the small city welcomed the eccentric as well as it accepted the varied social classes that were the cornerstones of its character, a place where the descendants of the original wealthy were still called founding fathers. In Daisy's hometown the farmers and ranchers were often land rich and cash poor; the elderly managed to live in their own homes through their eighties and nineties, while the young left Guthrie to work in Stillwater, Norman, Edmond, and Oklahoma

City. There was little industry in Guthrie, something Kenneth felt hurt its economy. He hoped this would soon change.

While many businesses in Guthrie were successful because they focused on tourist trade, Daisy's Rose Nursery and Garden Shop was successful because Daisy was a true hometown girl. She was born and raised in Guthrie, was respected and well liked in the close-knit community, and when she'd opened her doors for business, the locals had flocked to her garden center in numbers so steady that she'd opened in the financial black and stayed in the black.

She stayed in the black because she focused on service and quality merchandise. Whenever possible, she offered expert gardening tips to her customers and concentrated her business on flowers that thrived in Oklahoma weather and flourished in the red, heavy clay soil that dominated Guthrie land, Logan County land.

Kenneth recognized that the same care and dedication Daisy brought to her business, she brought to their relationship. She spread praise like fertilizer, hope like water, and whenever a problem surfaced between them, she tackled it the way she tackled challenges in her gardens— by examining them objectively and then ridding herself of them quickly and systematically until only the beauty, or at least the promise of beauty, reigned once again. He admired her tenacity, her willingness to go the extra mile. It was a trait they shared.

In turn, Daisy was content to rest in the seat

beside Kenneth. She was usually closed on Sundays, but she often did a spot check of the gardens, just to make sure everything was okay. Sometimes unwanted birds or small critters made their way into the nursery and she liked to keep caterpillars from eating the leaves of flowers designated for sale. In this way, she kept her wares in optimum condition.

She was glad she had made no plans to tend the garden shop the following day so that she could enjoy two full nights alone with her love before she returned to her regular daily routine of running her business. Daisy's Rose Nursery and Garden Shop. Just seeing the hand-lettered sign made her proud.

Located on South Division in Guthrie, United States Highway 77, the garden shop served as Daisy's oasis, a place that was neutral because it brought together people from all age groups and walks of life, from young stay-at-home mothers to weekend gardeners to retirees. She rarely felt her job was a burden. Instead, she thrived in her chosen profession.

In this regard, Daisy's work complemented Kenneth's work, which also dealt with people from all age groups and walks of life. A private investigator, he specialized in missing persons cases, although he often gathered information for insurance companies or provided security background checks for employers, dignitaries, athletes, and entertainers.

Very little of his work was hazardous, most of it involving elementary deduction, common sense reasoning, and attention to detail. On the odd occasion he needed extra help, he hired it and billed the client. Daisy operated on a similar level. She hired extra hands when needed, mostly during peak seasons.

In the companionable silence of the truck, Kenneth felt an odd sense of peace when he crossed from Oklahoma County into Logan County, where Daisy lived. He registered the bumpy road, and the feel of Daisy beside him, her hand resting suggestively near the apex of his thighs, the tip of her index finger caressing him in a slow absentminded type of rhythm.

Because she trusted him behind the wheel, she was able to relax, her head resting against the passenger seat, her eyes closed as she listened to George Benson playing on the stereo. The song they listened to was called "I Just Wanna Hang Around You" and the words the aging jazz guitar player sang were just right.

Inside the truck's cab, the smooth jazz between them, it was easy to imagine their hearts beating as one, that their minds were filled with thoughts of each other. The mood spelled anticipation, a feeling shared by both.

Kenneth wished they could stay together in Daisy's house until they ran out of food and other necessities. Thinking about her responsibilities, he asked, "What exactly will you be doing for this show you're having?" She had a regular work week scheduled, in addition to running her first garden show.

She sighed, as if she was reluctant to break

her restful silence with talk about her job. Still, she understood why he asked. He was right to ask. She believed communication was nine-tenths of a long and satisfying relationship. They needed to be clear on how much playtime could be carved from her work schedule. The spring and summer seasons were her busiest times of year and it was never easy for her to gain free time. This week was an impossible one for Daisy.

She said, "First of all, this show is strictly for amateurs. We'll be focusing on living plants. We'll have judges and teachers of miniclasses in horticulture as well as news media coverage. It's a big deal, bigger than I first expected." It had snowballed from the idea phase to its final exe-cution and props still had to be made. Thinking of everything she had left to do before the event made her tense, her earlier euphoria quickly disappearing.

"Will there be any cosponsors?" Kenneth asked. He was surprised at how involved and serious the show had turned out to be. It sounded as if it would be a major event, and for the first time, he realized that he hadn't really been listening when she'd updated him on her plans prior to this visit. He'd been caught up in his missing persons case.

He wanted to be supportive but he actually wished Daisy had nothing so specific planned for the week. He had known she would be busy, but not as busy as it now sounded as if she would be. He supposed he should be grateful that she'd made the time to pick him up from the airport at all. She had to be tired from planning and organizing the flower show while running the garden shop full-time. No longer kicked back with her eyes closed, she was staring out the window.

Daisy was silent because she was thinking. She'd noted the shift in Kenneth's attitude, from being slightly edgy from his travel to being alert about the details of her business week. She knew he was calculating the opportunities they'd have to be alone before he returned to Wichita at the end of the week. "No," she said finally, "but the newsletter going around features advertising from my vendors."

"The people you get your own supplies from?"

"Yes, like my bags of mulch, my seeds and also the pottery that's sold in the shop," Daisy said.

Kenneth took his time to think about her response. In doing so, he was able to visualize what she'd be dealing with and how he might be able to help her achieve her goal of a successful event. In order to help, he needed to understand the various parts of her upcoming program. "Do you have categories of flowers or something like that?"

"Yes," Daisy said, pleased he was interested. He could easily have made life difficult by demanding more of her time than she could reasonably allow; people depended on her for guidance.

It was tough enough to squeeze a romantic interlude between her regular business and the side business of the garden show, but it would have been extremely tiresome to deal with a negative attitude from the man she loved.

For the most part, she and Kenneth were so compatible that she sometimes worried if what they shared was too good to be true under everyday conditions. This week would be a great proving ground. With fried nerves all around them, their generous natures would be tested, both in public and in private.

She said, "The competition for the roses is broken down into tea rose specimens, climbers, ramblers, floribundas, and minis. Each area has a class taught by one of my gardening club members. We'll all be very busy on the day of the event, but because of all the planning we did in advance, we feel prepared for whatever happens. Unless something freaky goes down, the garden show should be a success. Besides, from start to finish, the event should last for the morning only. We can all hang for that long."

Kenneth nodded his head. Daisy and her friends were taking the time to work out foreseeable trouble spots so that when the garden show was presented, the garden club members would be available for questions, answers, and education. Leave it to Daisy, he reasoned, to cram a lot into a very short time. She thought and worked in a concentrated format.

He expected that her one-day flower show

would be unforgettable. How could it be anything else when its hostess was throwing her entire body and soul into the project? Kenneth figured he had a lot of catching up to do if he planned to help her keep the event fluent and trouble-free.

"So," he said, "those people who want to know more about climbers and ramblers can learn about them as opposed to learning about the tea roses?"

"Yes."

Daisy loved it when he came to visit, when he treated her as if she was the only person in the world who mattered. His presence filled every room with his own special brand of masculinity. In the truck, his confidence allowed her to let her own guard down. Soon they would be home, at her place.

There, in the bedroom, his shoes would rest enormous next to hers, his presence again reminding her of how good it felt to share her life, however briefly, with a man able to ease the ache of far too many nights spent alone. Soon they would have absolute privacy.

He blended his life to hers easily on the surface, when in truth, he worked hard at getting along, at protecting a relationship he valued. In his line of work, Kenneth had learned to take nothing for granted, but it was the little, unconscious things that endeared him to her during his many brief, intense visits.

At the table in her kitchen, he ate twice as much as she did, which she found funny. In their downtime, he preferred to watch sporting events on television while she turned the set to the Home and Garden channel or to a channel that featured classic films. She relished their differences. It was hard to imagine life without him.

Over six feet tall and two hundred pounds, single and childless, Kenneth excelled in his career as a private investigator, a part of his life that he generally sheltered her from by not talking about it.

As far as Daisy was concerned, the only problem with his career was that his business was located in Wichita, Kansas, a profitable location for him. As much as she wanted him near, she had never asked him to make the sacrifice of relocating, one she knew she couldn't make herself. Guthrie was home and always would be.

Kenneth had been tempted to relocate to Guthrie in order to be closer to Daisy but had not given in to the impulse. He was not a rash person; there were definite signs that he should tread forward in their relationship on slow but steady feet. Daisy wanted her own space, and no matter how many times he asked her to marry him, she refused.

She refused because she believed that marriage was a lifetime commitment. She was afraid of making a mistake, something that would be easy to do in the company of such a charismatic man as Kenneth, a man who found part of his attraction in the fact that she was not immediately accessible to him on any given day. Distance, for him, added flavor to the pot.

She was one of those people that believed absence made the heart grow fonder, and while it was true that she cared deeply for Kenneth, it was also true that she believed marriage would diminish the ultimate authority she held over her own life: she would forevermore think in terms of two instead of one, his opinions and feelings as well as her own. Life would no longer be simple.

It was much easier to focus on her own wants and needs within the comfort of the home and business she'd built for herself. . . . It was the beautiful sense of companionship, of oneness, that she could never duplicate without Kenneth. It was that scrumptious singular way she felt when they were alone together, like now, that let her know he was more than too good to be true; he was a definite keeper.

Still, fear of failure was in the back of her mind, a reality check that kept her grounded. Beautiful things were sometimes broken. She was strong on her own, but once she fully opened herself and her life to include Kenneth, would she be as strong if he changed his mind about them, if he left her someday? It was a leap of faith she wasn't ready to commit to.

She enjoyed the electrifying shot of energy she received every time he stepped off the plane and into her waiting arms. The only other thing in her life with the ability to make her nerves jangle was coffee, something she drank at least a dozen times every day. She liked her coffee hot, black, and strong, qualities she also attributed to the only man in her life.

Kenneth made her feel treasured and desirable, whether she wore make-up or not, had on jeans or a sundress. He and coffee were her two favorite vices. She wondered how her lover would feel if he knew that she considered her growing devotion somewhat of a blemish on what had, until now, been an easygoing lifestyle. To be her own boss in every way was, for Daisy, a true turn-on. She excelled with power.

Her business was successful because she put her heart into the running of it. Kenneth diverted that energy from the business to himself. In the past, nothing and no one had been allowed to interfere with the running of her garden shop. The way caffeine kept her addicted to coffee, power kept her addicted to business, and now, love kept her addicted to Kenneth Gunn. To date, she hadn't been able to get enough.

Once they arrived at her house, they quickly settled into the kitchen, their usual way to transition between whatever he'd been dealing with before visiting and whatever she was putting aside to make room for him. It was a neutral zone.

At the kitchen counter, Daisy filled a paper filter with fresh ground gourmet coffee. The day before, she had bought whole beans from D.G.'s Coffee, a two-story turn-of-the-century brick building in Guthrie, something she did every other week as a special treat for herself. Since she and Kenneth were going to sit on the porch for a while, Daisy put the coffee in commuter mugs. This way the coffee would stay hot in a container that was easy to carry around.

Kenneth always liked to walk through Daisy's gardens to see her current projects, something he'd do first thing in the morning. Over the last six weeks, she'd been working on a cottage garden that was crammed with annuals and perennials.

His favorite thing to do when she planted a new garden was to look for garden follies, little yard ornaments she tucked away in the flower beds. Since his last visit, she had set toad houses on the ground, one beneath a perennial rudbeckia and one beneath a biennial foxglove, something he'd noticed because of the bright security light outside near the place he'd parked the truck. His deep interest pleased her.

"I love June," Daisy said. It was clear from her tone and body language that she loved Kenneth in June, as well.

"Me, too," he said as he gazed through the windows in her casually decorated white kitchen. Everything about Daisy's home and life was casual, and yet the way she put it all together made her home and her life as gratifying to Kenneth as old-fashioned comfort food: meat loaf and mashed potatoes, fried chicken and collard greens. "Your gardens are like pictures in a magazine. I've never seen anything like them."

"Thank you. By now, you know how much I

like theme gardening. It's a great way to experiment with patterns and colors."

Kenneth smiled at her. "You've definitely done that."

After the modern feel of Wichita, Kenneth always enjoyed the stepping-back-in-time feeling he got whenever he returned to Guthrie, a city that focused more on renovation of existing properties than the construction of new ones, a habit that helped to make the city charming and unique.

He hoped the city would continue to grow tastefully and gracefully. He expected this because its neighboring city, Edmond, was creeping into traditionally rural areas. He and Daisy enjoyed Sunday drives through the new neighborhoods, homes that were edging toward the main city of Guthrie.

Daisy believed the town was changing for the better, slowly, but definitely changing. There were children who spent many years away from home only to return to Guthrie to settle and retire, bringing with them the knowledge and skill they had learned from other parts of the country and the world.

She believed that those returning were the town's anchors because they remembered the good times, the days when there was more than one public swimming pool, more than one movie theater, and many things for all ages to do, from shopping to living to recreation. It was Daisy who pointed out that Guthrie was becoming a mecca for artists with talents ranging from music to painting to sculpting and in her case, gardening.

She approached gardening as a form of recreation and as an art form, which was one of the reasons her gardening club was such a success and why her rose nursery and garden shop had become a tourist attraction: Daisy helped customers choose gardens to fit their home landscape designs. This work was a natural extension of her own home landscape designs.

When she did this, she considered climate, topography, and how the yard space would be used by a given family. For example, front yard gardens tended to be more formal and neighborhood friendly than backyard gardens, which tended to meld with the natural habits of the family that lived in the house. This proved a successful strategy, one that increased word-of-mouth business sales and repeat customers.

Kenneth believed that there were no two homes exactly alike in Guthrie, even though many shared the same type of window casements or basic design structure. This was definitely not a cookie-cutter-styled town.

Overall, what Kenneth saw in this part of central Oklahoma was opportunity. A man could make his mark and have it stand for generations. Daisy had done this with her business.

While it was true that many people planted vegetable gardens or planted crops, there were some Guthrians who planted flowers simply for pleasure and recreation. Daisy was one of those gardeners, and from what Kenneth had seen from his drives around town, her gardens were spectacular.

Her gardens were exceptional because they fit perfectly with her home, so that outside gardens became extensions of the rooms inside her house. Guests like Kenneth were made to feel as if they had found some sort of harmonic living zone that was free from personal problems and public politics.

At Daisy's place, more than beauty reigned supreme; there existed a profound state of tranquillity, as if being on her property was in some way a commune with nature so wonderful that it bordered on a personal meditation.

For him, this setting was a much-needed respite from his daily life. It was no wonder she chose not to move away from Guthrie. Daisy was one of those people who turned her house and property into a private oasis, a verdant place that satisfied nearly all her needs. Kenneth felt welcome.

The feeling started with Daisy's home itself. It was a 2000-square-foot country-styled farmhouse complete with a porch that ran the length of the front of the house. There was a detached double-size garage that had a red climbing rosebush sprawled along the east side. The house was painted yellow with white trim. White shutters bordered more than a dozen windows. The roof was tiled in blue. No other home in Guthrie came close to this one.

Daisy's home was the only classic farmhouse with this particular set of colors. Built in 1900, the floors and house were made of wood. The rectangular shape of the house ran north and south, the entrance door facing west. The setting was friendly and the front yard overflowed with flowers that bloomed from spring until fall. Seldom did her yard have nothing in bloom.

There were huge drifts of perennial and bulbs that were interspersed with annuals for variety and sharp contrasts of color. The overall mood of the house was neighborly and very relaxed. The driveway and walkways near the house were curved and made of either brick or stone. There was no cement visible anywhere on the grounds. Even the foundation of Daisy's house was made of old stone.

Huge trees afforded the house seclusion from the highway it faced and provided protection from the setting sun. There was a short picket fence on either side of the driveway and in front of the matching fences were lavender shrubs, a group of four-foot-tall foxglove, and white iceberg roses that smelled divine, even in the dark.

On the outer sides of the picket fences were weeping willow trees, their bottom fringes trimmed evenly above the ground so that when Daisy manicured the lawn on her riding John Deere mower, she didn't have to duck her head. The other benefit of trimming the willow trees was to make sure that sunlight reached the iceberg roses, which needed at least half a day of sun everyday.

However, it was the gardens, not the color scheme, that set Daisy's home apart from every other home in Guthrie. She used theme gardens as a way to experiment with color and placement. Her songbird garden was composed of circular shapes that created an intimate setting from the house and other gardens.

There was a white bistro table with two chairs set beneath a mature dogwood tree that had lovely pink flowers when in bloom. On the table, in a decorative tin box, were two binoculars, a pair for Daisy and a pair for a friend if she had one visiting with her.

The binoculars were used to study the birds in the natural habitat she'd created for them. In the songbird garden, there were birdbaths, a rotting log for woodpeckers to play with, hummingbird feeders, nectar-rich plants, and plants that produced edible berries. It was a songbird's paradise.

For relaxation, Daisy and Kenneth often sat in the songbird garden to listen to the birds sing or to watch them play, a habit Kenneth had come to look forward to during his visits. There was a small grass garden that was made of ornamental grasses, which Kenneth would have called weeds until meeting Daisy.

She had an English garden, its focal point a classic-style gazebo. The large yard feature had a single entrance and was distinguished by its simple and traditional pattern, a configuration composed of eight sides and an overall area of roughly 160 square feet, just enough room to seat ten people comfortably.

Inside the gazebo was a white wrought-iron

table set. All the furniture in Daisy's garden was white, the color she preferred to showcase her flowers and the subtle background of green grass. White was also phosphorescent in the twilight hours. For those reasons, Kenneth was able to enjoy her gardens by using only the light of the moon, which always seemed brighter there, in the country feel of Daisy's gardens.

In turn, Daisy watched Kenneth catalog the subtle changes to her home since his last visit. One thing she liked about him was his ability to be strong without being a know-it-all bully. He knew a lot, but he didn't force his opinions or his attitude down her throat. He listened and he allowed her to talk whenever she wanted to say what was on her mind.

When she looked at Kenneth, she clearly saw his twin personality traits of absolute courage and absolute self-control. This was power. As always with supremely self-reliant people, there was the negative side of power, the ability to ruin what was created in the first place. A man like Kenneth was his own best friend or his own worst enemy.

Coming from a sound family background and normal upbringing, Kenneth was secure and emotionally stable. He was rugged, naturally charming, and confident. She enjoyed his take-charge attitude and appreciated the way his sense of humor kept him from being overbearing.

His empire was his private detective agency and his Achilles heel was his habit of performing pro bono work for people he considered underdogs, those who were weak or perhaps just temporarily down on their luck.

In this regard, Kenneth was like Daisy, whom many claimed had a bleeding heart. Daisy took in stray animals, mostly cats and dogs, fed them, and took them to the animal shelter if there was no matching description for the animal in the lost-and-found section of the *Guthrie News Leader*, her hometown newspaper.

"Found any new strays lately?" Kenneth asked. His tone was teasing.

She rolled her eyes. People sometimes delivered stray animals to her door when the shelter was closed. Kenneth had witnessed this once and had been asking her this question ever since. "No."

He leaned over and kissed her, just because he loved her. "I've always wondered how you manage to keep Cutie Pie from getting jealous of the time you spend with other animals." Cutie Pie was Daisy's four-year-old German shepherd, a big dog with black-and-nearly-white fur. Daisy had rescued the animal from a pet adoption service on a whim. She and the shepherd fell in love at first sight.

Daisy shrugged. "Cutie Pie knows that when I put a stray in the holding pen, it isn't permanent and that I'm trying to help. She might feel differently if I took on another animal full-time, but for the most part, she's secure and happy. I spend a lot of time with her."

Kenneth had seen them in action together.

The dog followed Daisy around the gardens to keep an eye on her. "It shows. She's very loyal."

"I'm lucky to have her."

Kenneth ran his eyes over Daisy's attire and thought, *I'm lucky to have* her. She wore a soft knit capri pantsuit in a light peach color. The fabric was lightweight and clung to her every curve. Her sandals were slim and gold. Her lipstick was a shimmery pink-red, her other make-up very light and complementary to her skin. She looked like a bloom on the flowering confetti lantana she grew at the base of her mailbox.

She smelled as delightful as she looked, yet it was her eyes, sharp and inquisitive, that held his attention. Her eyes were the windows into an intelligent mind. Right now, that energy was directed solely at him.

As much as he wanted to help her out of her pantsuit, he knew they had all night long to linger in each other's arms. One thing he never wanted to do was make her feel his main objective was to get her between the sheets. He wanted all of her, inside and out. They needed to finish off the parameters of this brief lovers' holiday. He said, "Tell me more about the garden show."

She chuckled softly over his ability to focus. This was not a man who rushed things, but rather a man who felt comfortable setting boundaries, who preferred not to mix business with pleasure. So did she.

She said, "I'm having it at the fairgrounds

here in town. Kandi Kane will attend and present awards. She's the keynote speaker."

Kenneth refilled their commuter mugs with coffee and turned off the electric pot. Even though they were planning to spend their night making love, he'd have been too wired to sleep anyway. He never could understand how Daisy was able to drink coffee at 10:00 P.M. and be fast asleep in bed by 11:00 P.M. "What a name," he said. "Kandi."

"Yeah, and believe me, that woman is anything but sweet."

Kenneth heard the disgruntled note in her tone and was curious. "Why are you inviting her, then?"

Daisy's shrug was eloquent. "She's a celebrity garden buff. A good word from Kandi Kane is like manna from heaven. Sales quadruple when she gives a green light on a business. That's a boon for a retail shop like mine."

Kenneth wanted to understand Daisy's reservations about the celebrity speaker. "Then what's the problem with her?"

"She's a terrible gossip. Nasty. She acts as if she's mad at the world or something, but she writes wonderful stories. I want one of those stories written about my business."

Kenneth was surprised this would be an issue for such a brief encounter. "What does she do when she's rude?"

"Kandi makes ugly comments about people's private lives and she dishes out personal details along with her garden column, which is regionally syndicated. When she wrote about the up-coming garden show in her column, she mentioned that I took in a stray man last year, a man I knew nothing about and kept all to myself until he was feeling better. She made it seem as if I was daft and more than a little bit desperate."

Kenneth knew Daisy was referring to the way they'd met. Two thugs had beat him up and left him for dead in her garden. Unfortunately, his beating was severe enough to leave him unconscious, a condition that led to a brief bout of amnesia. Daisy had taken care of him until he'd recovered mentally and physically. His recovery had been complete.

Afterward, she had helped him solve the murder mystery he had been investigating before the beating. Since then, they had been engaged in a long-distance relationship. Kenneth was tired of the arrangement. He wanted more, needed more.

Even though she loved him, Daisy liked living on her own and wasn't in a hurry to change her lifestyle dramatically by getting married. This elusive quality about her kept Kenneth on his toes. He was obsessed with her in a way he'd never been with another woman. She wasn't playing hard to get—she really was.

Kenneth said, "Tell me more about Kandi Kane." He wanted to be armed in case the woman proved dangerous.

"Kandi is gorgeous. Dark-skinned, flawless complexion, supershort black hair that she curls tight to her head. She wears trademark boots she orders from Sorrell Custom Boots right here in town."

This startled him. "Kandi is from Guthrie?"

"No," Daisy explained. "She's from some little town in the middle of nowhere, but she met someone with a pair of Sorrell boots on and loved them so much she wanted a pair just like them."

Kenneth had never seen Daisy wear anything on her feet other than gardening shoes, tennis shoes, or the occasional sandals. "Do you have any of these boots?"

"I commissioned the artist to make me a pair of kangaroo boots in a design we worked out together. She's got a waiting list of customers but she expects to have my boots ready in time for Christmas. It's my present to myself."

"What's the design on your boots?"

"There's a cluster of daisies tied with a ribbon and on the ribbon are the words *Daisy's Rose Nursery and Garden Shop.*"

Kenneth shook his head and smiled while doing it. "Guthrie is full of newsworthy people. I don't think I've met a dull friend of yours yet."

"That's another reason why I like D.G.'s Coffee. No one is ever a stranger there and it's an unofficial haunt of artists."

Kenneth was silent a few seconds. "Is that where you bought the new birdhouse?"

Daisy's eyes lit up. "You noticed!"

"Of course. It's why I like to walk through your gardens whenever I come to visit. It lets me know what you've been up to and I like seeing the seasonal changes in your yard. The birdhouse is a nice addition to your porch ornaments."

"I think so, too. I had the artist coat the overall piece in a weather-resistant veneer since the front of my house gets so much sun."

The birdhouse was an octagon shape that the artist had crackled and painted an antique white. It had a purple-and-green vine painted on it and rested on an antique white pedestal that Daisy had nailed onto the porch to keep it from being knocked over by the wind.

On either side of the birdhouse were a pair of stark white rocking chairs made of wood. The cushions on the chairs had the same purple and green vines the artist had painted on the birdhouse. Items such as these made Daisy's place unique.

Kenneth said, "It all fits. Your hobbies and friends and favorite haunts are all connected into a circle."

Daisy hadn't thought about it before but Kenneth was right.

An artist himself, he had built a bench for Daisy that wrapped around the scarlet maple tree in her backyard.

"But it's more than that," he said. "You have a great eye for putting a variety of things together, mix-matched things. You don't just throw plants haphazard in the yard, you have a pattern and shape to what you do."

She smiled. "So do you. Speaking of pattern

and shape, why don't you go ahead and turn part of the garage into a workshop for yourself? You could make birdhouses to sell in the garden shop. They'd be a big hit. I'd sell them with packets of flower seeds known for attracting local birds. I can hear the cash register ringing now."

Kenneth laughed. "Just about everything you do gets somehow connected to your garden. The people you meet. The places you go. Everything. Maybe that's part of your success. You love what you do and you do what you love."

"Don't make me sound so cherry-pie sweet and so . . . organized. Basically, I just go with the flow. I can't stand Kandi Kane but I'm excited about what she can do for my business. If you could build birdhouses, I'd be able to premiere them after Kandi's big write-up in the papers. I'm already selling wind chimes and outside wall thermometers.

"There are people who want me to sell trees, but they take up too much space. I refer them to my friend Robin Brandon out on Highway 33. She refers people to me and so we help each other in business that way. Kind of like how D.G.'s Coffee and French Underground help each other."

Kenneth laughed at her. "You and your coffee. I'd hate to see what would happen to you if you tried to stop drinking it. Have you ever tried?"

"Once. I had a colossal headache when I did and I've never tried since. I used to drink Folgers coffee but then I sampled some gourmet coffee and got hooked. The more I drink, the more I want. That's how I think of you, too. The more time I spend with you, the more time I want to spend."

"Marry me."

"No."

"Don't you want children?"

"No."

"Don't you want me to be with you every day and night?"

"No."

"You're a tough cookie, Daisy."

She wished they didn't have to go this route, but like the business of the garden show, they had to discuss this, too. This was a conversation about their future. If they couldn't make a case for one, this might wind up being their last time together. Neither of them could afford to pour feelings into a bottomless pit.

"I'm happy," she said. "I don't believe a woman has to be married with children in order to feel good. I have a career and a marvelous lifestyle."

"So if it ain't broke, don't fix it." He wasn't being nice.

"Right."

He stared her down, as if he dared her to deny the truth. "I know you get lonely some nights. One day we'll be old, Daisy."

"I'll be ready when the time comes and I'll feel good knowing I lived life on my own terms and that in the process I made other people happy along the way. Live and let live, that's my motto."

He frowned at her. "I could walk out of your life right now and you wouldn't protest, would you?"

She folded her arms across her chest. "Of course I'd protest, but I don't want you here unless you want to be here. The harmony you feel when you come to my place is because I don't fight the flow of things in life. What is, is. Like a friend of mine says, heaven and hell happen every day of our lives. We can choose to be happy or miserable. I tackle one day at a time and in that one day, I do my best to be happy. When I'm happy, it makes other people happy."

Her honesty hurt but it was real. "You keep life uncomplicated. I suppose that's the other thing about you that I find attractive after the hustle of Wichita. It's that black or white style of thinking of yours that intrigues me. You don't deal in gray areas."

She forced her breathing to even out. Communication was one thing, fighting was something else. She didn't like to fight. "Gray areas are for people who straddle the fence. I'm not one of those people."

"Is that why you don't practice an active religious life?"

"God created the day and every day is good, even though on occasion bad things will happen in the course of any given day. I don't sweat over things I can't control, which is everything outside my body and mind. I don't want to own you and I don't want to be owned by you. That's why I won't marry you, Kenneth."

The idea was like a chip on her shoulder, a big one. "Daisy," he said, "marriage isn't ownership."

"It is."

"Break this down for me because I totally disagree."

She expelled her breath in a huff. "You automatically get half of everything that is mine and the same goes for me with whatever you have. Marriage means we own the right to see each other naked, happy, sad, or whatever before anybody else does. It means you'd own part of my time and part of my space. I like my time. I like my space."

"You're talking about freedom," he said, seeking clarification.

"Yes. I like my freedom. I like being in a relationship with the front door open."

He rocked back in his seat. "Chicken."

She unfolded her arms and placed her elbows on the table. "Maybe. But why is it okay for a guy to be single forever and not a woman? Why is it okay for a man to choose a career over children and not be considered selfish or a freak of nature the way some women are?"

"I don't know, Daisy. I just know that being married means I alone would have the right to call you mine—and no other man. I want that right."

"See? You'd own me."

He thought she was being ridiculous about this ownership business and it showed on his face. "Maybe we should talk about this later."

"I won't be changing my mind."

"Anything is possible."

"I suppose if I can get Kandi Kane down here to little old Guthrie, then you're probably right."

His grin was lopsided, half serious, half not. "You've got a real knack for turning lemons into lemonade."

She batted her lashes like film diva Mae West. "You mean this weird conversation we're having?"

She really was being ridiculous. "We're having a fight. A controlled fight, but a fight all the same. I want to get married and you don't."

"It ain't broke," Daisy said, referring to their nearly year-old relationship.

Kenneth took her by the hand and pulled her outside to the bistro set in the songbird garden. He needed fresh air before he said something he might regret. A lighted path led their way. It smelled lovely in the dark, like roses and lemons and peppermint, things he couldn't see or touch without the sun to guide him. They held hands. "Tell me about this garden show and what I can do to help."

She was relieved to change the subject. "We'll need platforms and tables set up. Mostly, I'll need help with crowd control after the initial muscle part is over with."

"Muscle part as in lifting and hauling?"

"Yes. I'd also like a few plywood tables made with two-by-four legs that I'll cover with white plastic. Exhibitors will be able to showcase their specimens on them."

"So you need a carpenter, too."

"Exactly."

Kenneth liked to wear black the way fictional private investigator Kinsey Millone wore jeans, sneakers, or boots with a tank top or turtleneck as all-purpose gear. Black kept his travel bag at a minimum and his clothing always interchangeable. If he went to a restaurant after a day of work and had on a black top with black jeans, he could switch the jeans to black slacks and come out all right. Black would be a problem if he was working with wood and sawdust.

To save packing time and hassle, he kept a set of clothes at Daisy's place, so he knew he'd be able to find something more suitable for carpentry work. The issue of what the garden show would involve and how he could help now resolved, Kenneth was ready to end the evening in Daisy's arms. Their walk through the garden was the perfect segue.

The songbird garden was in full serenade and he marveled at the sounds. He admired the woman who'd created such a space from her own hands and imagination. Kenneth suppressed a sigh of frustration. He was in love with a woman who refused to marry him, a woman who didn't want children, a woman who didn't need a man to validate her self-worth, a woman he couldn't get out of his mind.

The chaste kiss she'd placed on his lips after he walked off the airplane was like the first lick of his favorite ice cream. One lick was not enough. He used his tone of voice to tell her he wanted to lick her from head to toe. "I was exhausted before I got here. I drank coffee on the plane to jazz myself up, but seeing you for the first time in six weeks is like mainlining six shots of espresso."

Daisy laughed. "Espresso makes my hair stand on end."

Kenneth laughed, too. "You drink so much coffee as a rule that it amazes me you can't drink espresso."

"Me, too. But every time I try it, my skin crawls with the willies and the hairs on my arms stand up."

He said again, just as he pulled her close within the circle of his arms, "We're gonna be up all night."

While Daisy and Kenneth did the wild thing between hot and sweaty sheets, Kandi Kane was psyching herself up to be the main attraction at Daisy's grand garden show special event. She, too, stood over a garden—a courtyard full of weeds. In the morning, she'd drive to Guthrie. In the morning, she'd have a pot to stir, people to rile, nerves to shatter. She only wished she had a more earthshaking name to go with her current hard-core attitude.

Kandi hated her name but she loved her

mother so she never changed it. Instead, she did everything she could to deny the manufactured sweetness her name implied. She was tough, smart, considered a bitch by many of her peers, but what she lacked in the way of true friends she made up for in the way of accolades from prominent leaders in the professional garden community.

She knew her fauna from her flora, and her specialty was in the selection of rather obscure garden shows in the seldom-heard-of small towns that dominated the southwest and lower southeastern states. She agreed to do the Guthrie event for garden show novice Daisy Rogers as a favor to the friend of a friend of her daughter, Sugar Kane.

Sugar had attended Langston University in Langston, Oklahoma, where she'd earned a degree in business administration. While at Langston, Sugar had met and befriended one of Daisy's former employees, a handyman named Chester Whitcomb, a man whom Kandi had been shocked to learn, was arrested and recently convicted of murdering an undercover policewoman, a friend of Kenneth's.

It wasn't until after Kandi accepted the assignment to cover the Guthrie garden show that she and Sugar made the connection of Daisy with Chester Whitcomb. It was a small world and a place where Kandi had learned quickly in life that a woman could run from her destiny but she could not hide, a fact she was chagrined to discover when she named her only child a name as silly as her own: Sugar.

Quirky names ran in the maternal side of Kandi's family. Her own mother, whose maiden name was Flowers, was named Sunnie. Sunnie grew fields of sunflowers in various heights and colors, which she harvested and sold to flower markets and craft stores throughout the middle and eastern states.

Kandi had left the family home, gotten pregnant by a man named William Kane, IV, who ran off with his father's secretary, a former stripper named Bootsie who made sure Kandi knew of the affair by sending her a nasty video of herself and William having sex on his father's mahogany office desk. This was while Kandi was pregnant.

Kandi knew the baby she carried was a girl because she willed it to be a girl and she crooned all the time to her unborn daughter saying things like, "It's gonna be all right, sugar. I love you, sugar."

When her daughter was born in the company of Sunnie Flowers and the cabdriver they'd hired to take them to the hospital, a driver named Sugar, Kandi knew it was destiny, the reason she named her daughter Sugar.

She figured that as long as her daughter didn't marry a man with the surname Pie or Plum, she would be all right. As far as Kandi was concerned, destiny was at it again, which gave her more than fifteen minutes of serious thought, the reason she was staring at a weed-infested garden in the middle of the night. Of one thing Kandi Kane was certain: there were no accidents in life.

Two

Sunday afternoon

Daisy and Kenneth were sharing a swing beneath the shade of a redbud tree. Holding hands, listening to the sounds of nature, they were heavy into their own thoughts. As much as she liked to have a good time with Kenneth when he came to visit her in Guthrie, Daisy also liked to stay on track with her business. She accomplished this by focusing on her goals, those private scoring points that stemmed largely from doing whatever it took to keep her garden shop in the black. Kenneth was a serious sidetrack because whenever he came around, she just wanted to play, day and night.

In order to stay on top of business, she steered away from the distractions posed by the needs of other people. She was constantly invited to attend this function or that function, to speak at this group or that group, constantly asked to serve on tourist recruiting committees and fund-raisers. A popular woman in town, both in social and professional circles, her presence was often in demand.

If she'd joined every conversation or function to which she'd been invited, she'd weaken the energy required to stay on top of her game—the crafting of fine, custom gardens, the nurturing of sturdy, healthy plants, the education of a buying public who found her business a comfort and pleasure, which was, in turn, the external view of her own happiness. Kenneth made her feel good on the inside. Eyes closed, head resting against his shoulder, she squeezed his hand. He squeezed her right back, even though he, too, was lost in thought.

There was so much to think about.

Staying on track kept Daisy's days from running together and her seasons in order, kept her in touch with her personal values, her intuition, herself. For Daisy, this approach to living and working, this intense concentration on personal solitude and professional longevity was a meditation, a way of experiencing time in motion. Rarely was she frustrated against time because it moved too fast or too slow. For Daisy, time was time, infinite, real as air, soothing as water, never circular or linear. It just . . . was.

In this detached way of thinking, Daisy was able to satisfy her basic needs; seldom did she feel cornered and trapped by her work, which was why she chose not to wear a watch; clock watching tended to reinforce boredom, to dissect the day into its tiniest bits and pieces, forcing her to think about the precise movement of time rather than its overall flow.

Precise movement included the tedious

watching of seconds or hours, but the overall flow had to do with the general way she felt by the end of the workday, either pleasantly pleased by the repetitious work, terribly bored, or overwhelmed by exhaustion.

In this way, Daisy experienced time as a process versus an irritation. She wasn't rushing to get somewhere or meet someone or fill her life with people and things she didn't need. This attitude made it possible for her to start things from scratch, to build a sound future from the ground up, to live well and to live strong.

Thinking quietly and thoroughly, living thoughtfully, in harmony with her environment, enabled her to make solid choices, which in turn made her a valuable and wise friend, to herself and to those people she deemed necessary to quality living: her mother, Rita, Zenith Braxton, Cinnamon Hartfeld, Mr. Dillingsworth, her garden club and . . . Kenneth.

He alone interfered with the solitude Daisy so carefully constructed and carefully protected. He shifted her thoughts outward, away from herself as an individual to herself as part of a couple. As a couple, there were issues of possession to resolve, such as personal freedom, personal boundaries, personal power, personal air space, all that business about being one, when Daisy already felt one in herself.

She didn't feel like half a person and therefore she didn't need a man to make her feel whole. Like time, Kenneth was just . . . Kenneth. He was easygoing, protective, kind, attentive, hers for the asking, hers for the taking.

In his own right, he was a force to be reckoned with, not a man to be controlled or manipulated or made to bow down in a show of submission. His power was his and her power hers, as long as they both were careful. It was tough for Daisy to be careful when Kenneth so easily broke her concentration, as he did now, stroking her palm softly with the rough underside of his huge thumb.

Being so close beside him, having him around from dawn to dawn, made her think of sex and satisfaction, of laughter and fun times, a playmate instead of a helpmate. His friendship was an asset, something she wanted to keep and to cherish, which is why she made space for him in her life whenever he had time to spare.

Being with Kenneth stopped time for Daisy. She lost track of minutes and hours and days, which made her wary when she considered the future. She couldn't afford to become a clockwatcher because watching the clock would make her feel ordinary, when normally she felt very enlightened, empowered and fully alive, as tied to her work and her home as the name on the sign above her business, DAISY'S ROSE NURSERY AND GARDEN SHOP. It was her world, her strength, and until meeting Kenneth Gunn, her everything.

In her line of business, it was easy to get caught up in the miniplanet she'd created, the place where her work and her living zones operated side by side, the only separation between them the one she devised in her mind and enforced with her own free will. Nothing was complicated until Kenneth came along—not one thing.

Maintaining a simple, graceful lifestyle during the hustle of everyday life took subjective reasoning, supported by decisive, goal-oriented acts. This willpower allowed her to be independent and self-contained, a woman who wasn't needy, a woman able to give the best parts of herself without submerging her desires or her identity for the sake of someone else's happiness. For Daisy, this spelled success.

It took determination as well as risk to be a successful entrepreneur. Daisy wasn't one of those people who started businesses and sold them once the thrill of start-up was over. For her, Daisy's Rose Nursery and Garden Shop was her life's work, the thing she did to keep on living and thriving in a world where, for many, time moved too fast and good things were too easily replaced with better items the first minute better diversions came along.

Her life was more like an old-time garden, one that adapted to the ravages of weather, sometimes dying to the ground as a tree and reemerging as a shrub, or even a rose that began as a tea hybrid one year only to revert to its native state as a climber the next. A veteran or master gardener was gifted at adapting, at designing ways to help a garden flourish despite the adversity of insects, sun, wind, frost, and for-aging animals.

In Daisy's world, she was the master, the expert veteran, and she relished her ability to pick and choose from the best life had to offer. Right now, the best thing life had to offer her was Kenneth Gunn. The balancing act between being alone and being part of a couple was bittersweet.

In the garden, there was time to meditate on the real world, to gain insight into the meaning of dreams, a place to forge fresh ideas, to re-define and maintain self-control, to provide comfort to herself and ultimately to others, as she had done when she found and met Kenneth. It was hard to imagine almost a year had gone by since they'd first met.

Since then, her garden and their relationship had grown more beautiful, more strongly rooted. Roots served as anchors to the earth; they harnessed water, stored food, were essential to health and vitality, to prosperity. For these reasons, Daisy herself was rooted.

Her garden and her home were similar anchors and now, in Kenneth, she'd found fruit. He was firm of flesh, dark of skin, unblemished, and reminiscent of a Fuji apple—not too sweet, not too sour, just right. He wasn't ordinary, but neither was he exotic. He was just right—not too needy, not too dominating, but very much himself, in control, self-contained, loving and lovable, as committed to his lifestyle as she was to hers.

The trouble for Daisy wasn't in wanting Kenneth, but wanting to share her already-full and balanced life with someone else. Once she let him in, she would meld and merge with him, give some of herself and some of her happiness over to him. And then where would her business be? Certainly, it would suffer, because her attentions would be diverted, a little for herself, a little for Kenneth, and the rest for the garden shop.

Number one, her business, even though it was her hobby, was also her source of food on her table at home. Number two, regardless of how long she worked or how difficult the occasional customer turned out to be, her garden shop was generally an uplifting experience for her and the people she shared it with on a regular basis.

Her customers had become her companions, just as royal purple salvia was a nice complement to the perfect peach roses in her garden. Her customers had become her means for communication, her method of not truly being alone even if she was, on occasion, lonely in ways that a woman without a steady partner can be.

Most of her customers existed in the gray space of her life, the place where they were more than casual acquaintances but less than true friends. True friends dealt with the good and the bad, the laughing and the crying: the truth. Kenneth was this kind of friend, and Daisy was smart enough to realize that she didn't need to be married to him in order to hold on to that bond. All she had to do was be fair.

What Daisy worried about was territory. She liked her territory just the way it was, occasional loneliness and all. And the territory she liked best was simply herself. She wasn't one of those women who gave so much of themselves away that they had little left to feed their own souls. In herself, she felt complete, even without a husband, even without children. She had her business to thank for that peace of mind, her home, her dearest friends.

She rebelled when people said, "Just close up and leave early," when they wanted her to tag along to some social event that was spur-of-the-moment, and even though she would consider it, she rarely gave such proposals more than a cursory thought. Repeat business depended on her reliability.

She had set hours to keep, and by keeping those hours, she showed her clientele she was not a flighty person. When out-of-towners arrived to peruse her wares, they were disappointed to find upon arrival that she was closed. This is why she scheduled vacation during off-season months and kept constant open hours.

Besides, without money she couldn't maintain her independence or feed the occasional stray animals she rescued, or satisfy her other, more playful appetites. She enjoyed water rafting each spring and fall, attending indoor rodeo functions at the Lazy E, or simply puttering around the house she'd lovingly restored. Because her life tended to be orderly and predictable, she liked to invent challenges, the flower show being such an invention.

This flower exhibition fed Daisy's desire to show Guthrie residents that flower growing was every bit as satisfying and rewarding and beneficial to the community as growing vegetables was to local wholesalers.

In a town where vegetable gardens and farm crops outnumbered landscapes heavily populated with flowers, this was no small task. A successful event would lead to greater publicity for her rose nursery and garden shop as well as more public education regarding the healing qualities of flower gardening.

There were many people who didn't realize that pansies could be candied in sugar and used to decorate cakes, or that jam could be made from roses, that lavender kept bugs away from linens, or that chamomile eased tired muscles and put an end to headaches.

Education, she had discovered, was the way to encourage strictly vegetable gardeners to experiment with flowers, beginning by adding a few easy things to plant among their vegetable favorites, such as allowing clematis vine to stretch to the top of an obelisk set among the leafy green vegetable section of the garden.

The possibilities of beauty for the table and for the home, whether indoors or out, were absorbing to Daisy. This fascination is what captured and held those people who were skeptical, the elderly in particular. She liked winning new customers in the same way a gambler liked winning at slot machines—eventually, constant effort paid off.

There were many elders in her community who asked when she planned to stop playing around with her life and get down to some real business, such as graduating from college, raising a family, or getting a corporate job. Daisy brushed those comments aside with as much grace as she could muster. She wasn't playing around. She was for real.

She lived on twenty acres, which she owned outright. Her home and her business were paid for. She used cash for what she wanted and worked ten full months of each calendar year. She'd been to the Bahamas, had toured Europe, and had attended college just long enough to decide she wasn't cut out for the traditional road to success, which was entirely okay with her closest relatives.

Her mother had raised her to believe that she was born successful and that everything else in life was gravy. Daisy subscribed to this philosophy wholeheartedly and this style of thinking was the source of her professional satisfaction. As far as she was concerned, there was always more than one way to skin a cat, but the best way was to be true to her own God-given strengths and natural inclinations.

For starters, Daisy was a nonconformist. By dropping out of college, she had freed herself of the need to adapt to conventional standards.

Bringing this subject up was as volatile among her elders as the discussion of religion or politics, other topics she avoided whenever possible. For Daisy, the concept of "live and let live" was a personal anthem.

She performed both random and specific acts of kindness throughout her day, every day. She donated money and time to her community; she was civic-minded when it came to good causes, such as rescuing stray animals off the street and Kenneth Gunn from her garden; she attended her own affairs and stayed true to the positive way she was raised.

With steadfast determination, she steered clear of the issues she couldn't change and preferred to experience people as they were instead of the way she wanted them to be, which was why she enjoyed Kenneth so much: He functioned in the same way.

In business, she'd quickly discovered that sports and gardening and weather were neutral zones. She kept up with the growth and progress of Guthrie High School athletes and attended home games during football and basketball seasons.

She hung the blue-and-white Guthrie Blue Jay mascot in the window of her shop as a way to express her community pride. In this manner, she was able to converse with husbands who waited for wives in the garden shop, or vice versa.

Instead of renovating old barns and other outbuildings to store equipment on her twenty-acre site, she invested in sturdy structures she had custom-built to suit her needs, so when local residents gave her a hard time about squandering her days in the yard or whatever, she smiled quietly and then deftly diverted conversation elsewhere. She knew what she was doing, even if busybodies around her did not.

The only formal education Daisy had regarding horticultural training was the apprenticeship she earned at her mother's side. A seasoned gardener in her own right, Rita Rogers specialized in medicinal herbs as well as floribunda roses, the classic white iceberg roses being her favorites.

In turn, Daisy's mother had learned from her own mother, and together the three women traced their flower gardening heritage all the way to rural Alabama, where Daisy's great-great-grandmother Hattie made her living as a laundress by day and a root doctor by night.

As a root doctor, Hattie devised tonics from assorted flowers and herbs she managed to grow year-round and was a godsend to poor Southern families with little or no money for traditional medicine or professional doctors, especially during the Depression when so many families struggled to provide food and shelter for themselves.

As a result of her heritage, Daisy grew up with a deep understanding of nature, of the value of flowers for healing the body and for soothing the mind through their careful and systematic cultivation.

In the current generation, she excelled in plant growing as a source of beauty, and her specialty was not simply in growing roses for the garden or table, but helping homeowners build gardens that suited individual taste and lifestyle, a popular service for new home buyers in the fast-growing Edmond community.

During the winter months, she designed home gardens on her computer for potential clients. However, it was her own private gardens that launched her secondary and quickly growing career, that of a landscape developer for small garden sites.

Daisy approached landscape development the same way an interior designer set out to enhance and decorate a customer's home, which was room by room. A room in a garden was generally a section devoted to a particular theme, a hummingbird garden for example, a butterfly garden, or an evening garden composed primarily of white flowers and plants with silver foliage.

When Daisy was finished with someone's garden, her deft ministrations with color and scale often made a small yard seem larger or a large yard more cozy than it did before she'd started the project. Unfortunately, her business was growing faster than she could handle on her own. The subsequent loss of total control was frightening. She needed help and she needed it bad.

What she wanted now was a reliable builder to construct and install garden features such as gazebos, playhouses, and pergolas. Her chosen source had to be reliable, had to care about quality, had to believe in her work as much as she did, someone like . . . Kenneth.

She broke her reverie to eye him with open avarice and said, "I want you to go into partnership with me."

His face was a perfect blank, though his eyes gleamed with interest. "I take it from the calculating stare in your eyes that you're thinking along the lines of business," he said.

His tone was cautious. As far as Kenneth was concerned, Daisy was fanatical about her gardening habits. Her single-minded attention to detail and micromanagement left her competition in the dust, and while it was true that he greatly admired her, Kenneth had no desire to be her whipping boy. He'd much prefer a marriage partnership; that way they could keep the careers they'd been enjoying all along.

She registered his caution but stuck to her objective. Daisy liked to win. After careful selection of the battles she fought, she rarely lost a fight. She cracked her knuckles and squared her shoulders. Although she spoke calmly, her grin was unholy. "I am."

She was so much shorter and smaller than he was, Kenneth felt like laughing at her cocky demeanor. Instead, he humored her by asking, "Is this related to the garden show?"

"Kind of. I started thinking about it after you volunteered to build and set up the props I'll need for the program," Daisy said. She didn't mind him coming at her sideways. Just as long as he entered the discussion without turning her down flat.

Kenneth took a deep breath and let it out slowly. He was on the verge of squashing his true feelings, but that wasn't his style. Truth was everything and everything had its own place in time, including this fight. Delaying the conversation wouldn't make the subject go away. Although it wasn't his custom to do so, Kenneth sighed long and hard.

"Look, Daisy," he said, then skimmed a hand over the back of his head with a palm big enough to hold a basketball. "I don't want to spoil our fun by going into business. In my experience, partnerships between friends who stay friends are rare. I want to stay friends. While it's true that I find your work interesting, I don't see myself managing plants for a living."

Her dark brown eyes narrowed into contemplative slits. He'd been brief and to the point. She countered in the same vein. "Translation. You don't want to feel as if you're working for me."

"Damn straight."

She knew full well he had a weakness for pro bono work. Anybody who did that was a sucker for a good cause, and no matter how she sliced it, her cause was definitely good. She tried a different tactic. "That's not what I'm proposing."

It was his turn to narrow his eyes. He knew she wasn't about to give up. Even though she

sometimes appeared absentminded, evidenced
by the way she lost track of time in the garden,
he knew that when she focused, like now, she
was sharp and decisive. Formidable.

He said, "What exactly are you proposing,
then?" This time, his tone was more curious
than cautious.

"I want you to build garden features and let
me buy them from you wholesale," Daisy said,
fast, as if she thought he might interrupt before
she got all the words out. She should have
known better. Anybody able to sit on surveillance for hours at a time had enough patience
to listen to his girlfriend try to win him over in
a fight she had no intention of losing.

She had him hooked. He asked, "What exactly are you talking about?"

Daisy explained, "I want you to build small
bridges to use in water gardens, small playhouses that are made to look like miniature cot-
tages, small potting sheds and potting tables
with benches."

Kenneth's expression was an odd mix of interest and skepticism. "You really think there's
a market for that sort of thing?"

"I do," she said. "Many of my customers ask
me for those types of follies for their gardens.
Recently, a woman asked if I could connect her
with someone who knows how to build a miniature gazebo to go with her daughter's play-
house."

"I wouldn't be interested in owning a full-
scale business," Kenneth said. A night owl by

nature, he could conduct such a business after hours, sort of like a hobby. What she proposed could be done.

"I understand," she said. "It would mean cutting down on your P.I. work."

"Not necessarily," he admitted. "Just say I do go along with this idea of yours and I do start a business in Guthrie. It would take a lot of capital to get going."

He knew what he was talking about; he was an excellent carpenter. One reason for this was because he paid attention to the details of craftsmanship. A major detail was the use of quality building materials. At best, such supplies were costly. He couldn't afford to waste money.

She was getting excited and didn't care if it showed. "Okay. Good point. What if you worked on commission only? That way, you'd have start-up money for each project up front, like the retainer you get from a client to cover expenses once you start an investigation."

She had him there. "You've given this a lot of thought," he said.

"I have."

He sought some clarification on a subject that was near and dear to his heart. Other than sex with Daisy, it was the second major topic on his mind. "You still don't want to share a home together." He made this a statement, not a question.

"No."

He applied reason to their argument. "For an easygoing woman, Daisy, you're pretty stubborn on that issue. It would be simpler to live in the same house."

"Simple isn't always better," she countered. "I like having my own space, Kenneth. I like living alone. Besides, regardless of what you say, I know you like living alone, too."

He rubbed his chin with rough fingers, then lifted a brow in subtle agreement. "Living alone has its good points."

Daisy had spent a lot of time considering the pros and cons of maintaining a long-distance relationship with Kenneth. "For the price of your condo, you could buy a small house in Guthrie. I have plenty of land space and an out-building in the far back I use only for storage. We can clear it out for you to use as a studio. That way, you don't have to transport whatever you build and you can build whatever you want.

"Your work will always be on display and the gardeners who visit my shop will be able to see what you do. For you, it'll be free advertising. For me, it's a painless way to expand on my business. In your downtime, you can build things that are ready to go and sell. I've got a number of people interested in Adirondack furniture. I'm one of those people."

Kenneth's brain was ticking away at full speed as he considered the options Daisy presented so matter-of-factly. She was definitely a force to be reckoned with, all 120 pounds of her.

He could relocate to Guthrie and make a living doing the woodwork hobby he loved. As far as he knew, he would be the only person doing that type of work in town on a regular basis—a tempting thought.

Potentially, commissioned work could be done for anyone in the state of Oklahoma. Daisy's business would do the selling, he would do the building, and the customer would do the hauling off. "You make it all sound so easy," he said.

She tried to still her delight, lest he thought she was gloating, which of course, she was. "It is."

Kenneth said, "Just stop what I'm doing in Kansas, relocate to Guthrie, and start a new business doing something as risky as making big dollhouses for little girls to play in with their friends?"

"That's exactly what I'm saying. You keep telling me that you want us to be together all the time. We can. You'll be able to do your thing and I'll be able to do mine. Our businesses would complement each other and not contradict. We'd each have our own space. I like that idea. Also, we'd be on hand to help each other out if we need to."

Kenneth laughed. "You mean, you'll hammer and glue right along with me? Kind of like a hired hand?"

"Sure. Just like you'd be around to help me with the heavy work in my garden when I need it. Variety is definitely the spice of life."

Realistic by nature, Kenneth maintained a practical approach to the discussion. "It's still risky, and working with the public as an artist is a very uncertain business."

"Working as a private detective is risky. It's how we met in the first place," Daisy said, remembering how Kenneth's enemies had beat him up and left him for dead in one of the compost piles in her garden.

She had rescued him, helped him solve a vicious murder case, and eventually fallen in love with him. They had been together ever since. It was June and time for Daisy to review her plans for the way she would spend her winter season.

Each winter, she renovated her business in some way, starting with a deep cleaning, progressing to reinforcement of the shelving, touching up whatever paint had been scuffed or scratched, and ultimately in upgrading her shelving, storage, and other methods of display.

The previous winter, she'd hired a local painter to create a mural of a rustic one-story cottage on the north wall of the garden shop, Thomas Kincade-style, surrounded by gardens so realistic, many of Daisy's customers said the flowers looked real.

In this painted garden, there were vines of purple clematis growing among the red roses. Very old and established wisteria framed the entrance to the cottage and a nearly impenetrable hedge of perfect iceberg roses nestled against the base of the house on four sides. Among the star jasmine that fell over the split-rail fence in front of the vintage white cottage was the artist's name, which was written in script so lavish in design, it was almost unreadable.

The same artist, a sixteen-year-old high school student named Regina, had designed Daisy's business cards. Daisy had commissioned Regina to paint a weeping willow tree with a pair of little black girls in ribbons and ponytails swinging on a board seat attached to the tree with honey colored rope.

The girls in the swing represented herself and her sister, Miranda. At age six, one year older than Daisy, Miranda had been hit and killed when she ran into the street to save a stranger's dog. A witness to the horrible accident, Daisy hadn't been able to help her sister, but she'd been able to save many dogs and other stray animals ever since.

Many people, including her mother, had expected Daisy to become a veterinarian. She hadn't. Saving strays was something she felt compelled to do, a sort of homage to her sister. However, it was her mother's garden and love that had saved Daisy. In her mother's garden, Daisy had been restored and made to feel whole.

Perhaps because it was the garden that fed her mother's own bruised spirit after the death of her eldest child, a death that had been the catalyst for the separation and eventual divorce between herself and Daisy's father, Templeton Rogers.

During her parents' separation and divorce, Daisy had built her first garden, without any help or guidance from her mother who was distracted at the time. That first garden had led to another, which in turn had led Daisy to meet Regina over the fence that separated their houses.

Regina, who had moved with her family from Coyle, Oklahoma, to Guthrie, had been sitting on a tree stump in her own backyard, sketch pad in hand, as she recorded Daisy's first garden, ripe now with age and full of scent and color, on paper.

Thinking of the mural now gave Daisy an idea for the winter season, even though that time of year was several months away. She would dangle wind chimes on the painted porch and place handcrafted butterflies among the foxglove that grew along the faux painted steps of the cottage.

That way, when customers admired the design and wanted to take something home with them as a reminder of their visit, she would be able to discreetly suggest wind chimes and butterflies, simply by displaying them so creatively. Daisy discovered that she sold more of her knickknacks when she showed customers how they could be used in their own homes and gardens.

Because of this sales strategy, she was convinced any work Kenneth designed in the way of garden ornaments would sell quite well, especially if the prices were fair and easy to manage by ordinary people, customers she wanted to come back to the garden shop again.

Now that Kenneth had arrived, Daisy was ready to get down to the hard business of carrying out a successful garden show event. Thankful her garden club members were as excited as she was about the upcoming garden show, Daisy was confident the event would be a huge success with local participants.

She had one member of the twenty-member-strong garden club oversee a specific behind-the-scenes function, twelve major parts in all. Zenith Braxton, a miniature rose buff and Daisy's best friend, was functioning as her assistant by overseeing the various flower show committees in general.

It was up to Zenith to make sure each committee had a responsible chairman and that the duties of each chairman did not overlap. To do this, she maintained constant contact by phone and in person, and, ultimately, she reported what she knew to Daisy. On the actual date of the show, Zenith would stay mobile, free from any specific responsibility other than troubleshooting unexpected problems.

Cinnamon Hartfeld was in charge of the schedule committee, a position that required both focus and strong creative thinking skills. Her primary responsibility was to keep track of general information distributed to the interested public, making sure the rules for each division of the flower show were followed and that the overall flower show was balanced.

Keeping it balanced meant that the various parts of the show were carried out with equal finesse. The flowers used were to be fresh and the right flowers for the season, meaning everything that showed was material that would flourish naturally at this particular time of year.

She made sure that exhibitors were fairly equal in experience, that appropriate space was available for material and for exhibitors and for spectators to move freely between the two. Cinnamon also made sure that the various committees stayed within their budget. Daisy relied on Zenith and Cinnamon the same way she relied on her own two hands: fully aware of their limits and confident in their capabilities.

Whitney Webb functioned as the staging chairman for the garden show and her duties began the moment she first pitched the idea of a garden show to Daisy. Whitney was an experienced gardener who specialized in formal gardens, which she kept in exquisite condition, a result of constant attention to flower head removal, weed control, and constant clipping to achieve the highly manicured look that suited her rather rigid personality.

She was responsible for overseeing stage setups and their eventual breakdown, of litter control, lighting, and emergency contingency plans. Whitney was so thorough that she'd submitted a formal drawing of the exhibition site to each committee head, the local police, and fire departments. She had even arranged to have the event videotaped.

Daisy put Mr. Dillingsworth in charge of the judging, which included himself and two other garden club members. He and Kenneth would do any serious lifting that needed to be done before and after the show.

Daisy would handle all publicity, hospitality, and was general girl Friday. She expected record sales at the garden center. She could hardly wait.

Pushing them back and forth in the canopy-covered swing, Kenneth felt her excitement, and even though part of him understood her passion, he also recognized her obsession. More than ever before, he was determined to put romance in the relationship by reminding her at every turn that he was the hard body in her private landscape.

Since meeting Daisy, Kenneth had become increasingly dissatisfied with his Wichita, Kansas, lifestyle. At thirty-eight, he was single, had never been married, and had no children. At six feet two inches tall and two hundred pounds, he was lean, fit, and in his prime, his ebony-colored skin still taut and fit.

His eyes were light brown and friendly. He missed little in the way of details. He distinguished himself among his peers by being both honorable and decisive. He had liked his solitary life just fine until he met Daisy. She had him thinking about organic gardening versus pesticides, watering during the day versus watering at night, and so on.

She made him realize how lonely his life had been, something he discovered when he returned home after meeting her for the first time. His bed, which had once been a source of solace after a long shift at work, had felt empty.

Since then, he'd been to Guthrie as often as time and his schedule permitted, not nearly often enough, which was why he seriously considered Daisy's proposal to work together, but in separate areas of her business. It was crazy enough to work—tiny gazebos for playhouses in a doting mother's backyard.

In the last year, Kenneth had been to Guthrie six times, and Daisy had visited him in Wichita once. He'd been a private investigator for ten years, after a five-year stint with the police department in Wichita, Kansas. He was well trained and well connected. Until recently, he'd been satisfied with his life.

Each time he left Daisy he felt restless, often edgy or even distracted, which in his line of work could easily prove lethal. A change in his lifestyle was necessary, something he was smart enough to realize, but reluctant to act upon without a solid commitment from Daisy.

He was ready to be fully committed to her, yet without the benefit of marriage or even an engagement, the reasonable part of Kenneth's mind didn't think it was wise to chuck a profitable business that was well established for a risky business creating whimsical art for use by Daisy's customers in their gardens.

It was his heart that had no sense of caution. His heart told him to trade his sometimes-dangerous lifestyle for the relaxed social setting that was Daisy's world. In her world, there were no guns or missing persons or long hours spent on surveillance. In her tiny little planet, there was . . . sanctuary, a world within a world.

He loved just thinking about her. At thirty-five, she, too, was single and had never had children. At five feet three inches tall, she was a delightful combination of soft skin and finely tuned muscles that tended to ripple when she walked.

She kept in shape by running with her dog, Cutie Pie, and doing most of the work in her various gardens herself. She generally wore her shoulder-length hair in a ponytail. Her healing spirit and sense of adventure appealed to his own brand of self-containment. Like himself, she was able to create her own system for happiness.

The trouble for Kenneth was that now that his priorities had shifted outward to include her, the issue of their long-distance relationship was a specter before him. It just wasn't practical; it was expensive and tough on them as individuals. He'd think hard about Daisy's proposal. It was either that or nothing at all

Three

Monday morning

Medium brown, five feet three inches tall, curvy and casually dressed, fifty-something Rita Rogers adjusted the pageboy wig she'd ordered from the Gold Medal catalog and smiled. She was very pleased with her daughter. In particular, she liked the way Daisy was handling herself during the stress of managing her first garden show, an event Rita hoped would put her daughter on the regional garden map in a big way.

Rita thought it was wonderful that Daisy had a guiding finger in every pie, that she directly handled all major and final decisions, that she was on hand to solve occasional disputes and was responsible for securing and presenting the upcoming awards. Whatever credit came her way as a result of the garden show event would be worthy and appropriate. Rita's face glowed with pride.

To see her child prosper on her own terms filled Rita with a quiet sense of satisfaction. For her, Daisy's success validated whatever sacrifice she'd made in life to be a fair and supportive parent. Rita believed her daughter's outlook was a tribute to her own self-expression and cultural refinement, a marvelous blend of humility and inner strength that had rendered both women beautiful lives. There was much to be thankful for and to appreciate.

"Daisy," Rita said as she settled herself at the kitchen table, coffee mug in hand, "just about everything you touch turns to gold."

Daisy's eyes crinkled at the corners when she smiled. "Only my mother would say what you just did."

Rita swung her gaze to her daughter's left, in order to regard the third person in the room, Kenneth. "I'm not the only one who thinks so. I bet he'd agree."

Sprawled in his chair, his stomach full of tender buttermilk biscuits and sausage gravy, Kenneth clinked coffee mugs with Rita and said, "I definitely do agree."

Daisy changed the subject with a careless wave of her right hand. While it was true that she was sometimes uneasy with compliments, by accepting them without falsely belittling them, she was soothed by praise without being spoiled by it. She credited her mother with this ability to stay grounded.

To shift the conversation away from herself, she focused on troubleshooting the garden show. "I'm worried about the level of competition going on between the people who signed up to participate. It's rough."

Kenneth shared her visions of melodrama and like Daisy, he wanted to nip problems before they got out of hand. "I overheard talk of sabotage when I stopped by Gus' Liquor Store to buy some white wine."

Rita's brows rocked up a notch. "Oh, really?"

Kenneth continued. "I heard Miss Myrtle saying to Miss Tilly that Kandi Kane took a bribe by one of the contestants to make her a winner in the garden show."

Daisy laughed in disbelief. She often considered gossip the number-one pastime in Guthrie, sports and religion coming in second and third. "Kandi will be there to report what she finds out. She's not there to judge and she has no way to influence who wins a prize in any of the divisions. There's no reason to bribe her."

Rita refilled their mugs with the last of the coffee. "What if Kandi took money on a job she really can deliver on—like, say, a personal article write-up in her column? It's syndicated across the country. Somebody could potentially get more than ten minutes of fame."

Kenneth was shaking his head in bewilderment at the deadly serious way some people were taking what he considered a frivolous function, a show for flowers. He was continually amazed by the differences in his and Daisy's lifestyles, differences that were highlighted by conversations such as this one.

Until meeting Daisy, he'd never given a thought to flowers being grown for exhibition, a hobby he'd discovered appealed to both men and women. He had much to learn in order to keep up with Daisy's constant community involvement. "This is a flower show." He spoke each word with emphasis. "Dirt. Pots. That kind of thing."

Daisy made a face at him. Obviously, he didn't know squat. "Winning first place is a big deal."

Kenneth was determined to be more than the muscle in Daisy's business operation. To do this, he had to be willing to ask the obvious and question the loose ends. How else would he figure out what was going on?

He spoke with care and with patience. "Miss Tilly and Miss Myrtle made it sound like someone's exhibit might be sabotaged in order to make a guaranteed first-place winner." The women were senior members of the garden club who also used the opportunity to give him the questionnaires Daisy would place on the registration table on the day of the garden show. The questionnaire, presently stacked on the counter with boxes of black Bic ballpoint pens, was as open and concise as Daisy. The form read:

THANK YOU FOR COMING TO THE FIRST
GUTHRIE FLOWER SHOW
HOSTED BY DAISY'S ROSE NURSERY
AND GARDEN SHOP!
1. What city and state do you live in?

_____

2. Did you have a good time?

_____

3. How did you hear about the garden show?

_____

4. How old are you? (Please circle one.)
            20–30   41–50
            31–40   51–up
Comments:

_____

_____

Rita saw him glance at the stack of question-naires and grabbed one in order to see the finished product. The half sheets of paper were white with bold black print. She said, "In gardening, there are no guarantees. Like this form, it's good to start with the basics and build from there."

"She's got a point," Daisy said. "Given the size of this town and the relatively small scope of the garden show, I agree with you, Mom. Besides," Daisy added with a grin, "in the end, the cheater would never live down the scandal if word of foul play came to light. A contest isn't good unless everybody plays by the same rules."

Kenneth realized Daisy was as competitive as she was practical. He dug for more information. "Tell me about Kandi Kane and her sidekick, Sugar. Are their names for real?" The women, he figured, must have taken a lot of verbal abuse in the form of teasing. He was a firm believer that names contributed to a person's development.

Strong names inspired strength and other names inspired bitterness. Candy and sugar could be both sweet and hard or sweet and soft. Too much of either could make a person sick. A woman might act tough to compensate for the sweet name or she might go with the flow as Daisy had done. Apparently, the snippy-sounding Kandi Kane wasn't sweet and perhaps neither was her daughter, Sugar.

As far as he could tell, Daisy actually fit her name. In nature there were many types of daisies but the one that came to Kenneth's mind had rays of white petals surrounding a disc of yellow, a sturdy and reliable flower that grew freely in the wild or in a gardener's carefully cultivated backyard. In Daisy's backyard, they grew beside her potting shed in huge terra-cotta containers.

She reveled in the dedicated way he embraced her life, as if he wanted to know all the secrets in her gardens, all the quirks that made her uniquely herself. "Yes," she said. "Since the competition was announced eight weeks ago by the garden club, sales have doubled during the week and tripled on the weekend."

Kenneth marveled that Daisy wasn't having performance anxiety. With all the garden show gossip and pre-event shenanigans, he was surprised she hadn't put off his visit to Guthrie. Her composure made him feel proud, and like

Rita, he smiled. "This Kandi Kane character must really be a celebrity in the garden world."

Rita put her mug on the table hard enough to make it thump against the wood. "She's a regular little bitch, is what she is."

"Mom!"

Rita humphed. "I heard she threw a temper tantrum in Wal-Mart because she had to wait in line like the common Oakie she isn't."

"Is that what she said?" Daisy asked. It always shocked her when high-profile people acted like idiots.

"Yep," Rita said. "Her daughter was reported as saying Kandi ought to be used to Wally World by now."

"Guess so," Daisy said, her manner thoughtful. She figured Kandi's nerves must have been stretched out to the max if she was letting her composure explode in a busy place such as Wal-Mart. The only major shopping place in Guthrie, for many residents, going to Wal-Mart was like going to the mall.

Clearly, Kenneth didn't have a clue about what Daisy and her mother were saying. "Wally World?" He felt like he was playing a new board game and was just getting the hang of the rules.

"Around here," Daisy said, "Wal-Mart is often called Wally World."

Kenneth laughed. "I love this town."

Rita cut him a calculated stare. "Why don't you move here? Abe's Real Estate has a house for sale or for rent on my block. It's a two-bedroom single-story bungalow with a detached

garage. If you don't like that there's a property
with acreage out on Midwest Boulevard that's
for sale."

Kenneth surprised Daisy by pumping her
mother for more details. "The Midwest Boulevard property is more up my alley. How long
has the house been on the market?"

"Less than twenty-four hours," she said.
"Sign went up this morning. Wood floors, fresh
paint inside and out. No fireplace but lots of
windows. No near neighbors and it faces the
golf course."

Rita was so happy to finally get a chance to
unload her research on house hunting in
Guthrie she could scarcely stay in her seat. She
was flushed with excitement. As far as she was
concerned, Kenneth Gunn would make an excellent son-in-law.

She liked the way he was a thinker and a doer,
a combination that made him a successful entrepreneur and private detective. He was the
perfect counterpoint to Daisy's feeling-oriented,
artistic personality.

By his forming an official, exclusive relationship with Daisy, Rita figured that Kenneth's
presence would keep Daisy from being so totally
immersed in her garden center. Unless she was
on vacation, Daisy rarely left Guthrie, and when
she did, it was seldom beyond the Oklahoma
City Metro limits.

Kenneth was fully aware of Rita Rogers's mo-
tives. He tapped his left index finger on the
table, once, twice. "What Realtor?"

"Lloyd Lentz. Their office is located on Division, right next door to the Walker Tire Company."

Kenneth ignored Daisy's look of chagrin at his continued interest in the property. He couldn't pinpoint its exact location even though he was familiar with the street, a red-dirt-and-rock-covered road that once took him from Guthrie to Edmond on a Sunday-morning drive with Daisy.

On that day, he'd accessed the road off Highway 33, going south on Midwest Boulevard. Along the way, he'd passed a golf course, ranch-styled homes on rural acreage as well as trailer parks and formal, traditional ranching properties. He was intrigued by the opportunity Rita presented him, one that incorporated his need to be near Daisy and her need to retain autonomy.

"Any way you can get me an appointment to see it?" he asked.

Grinning, Rita also ignored Daisy's surprised expression and wide-open mouth. "I'll get you in there tonight." She pushed her chair away from the table and stood up.

Kenneth understood where Daisy's instant decision-making process came from. Rita didn't waste time with small talk and she wasn't afraid to stick her nose in someone else's business when she felt it was necessary. Apparently, she was worried he and Daisy might not hook up if she didn't put her two cents on the table. "Morning's fine," he said.

Rita slung her purse over her shoulder, its leather soft from constant use and perfectly matched to the custom kangaroo boots she wore with nearly all her casual wear. "Tonight's better," she said, her manner efficient and matter-of-fact. "You can look it over again tomorrow if you like it. If you don't like it, well, then tomorrow you can look at something else."

Kenneth smiled. "I suppose you're right."

Satisfied with her matchmaking skills, Rita bid them both a hasty farewell, but Daisy followed her mother out to her cherry-red vintage sports car with its cream seats and matching rag top. There was no other car like it in Guthrie. The same English rose carved on her boots and purse was also painted on the hood of her car.

"Mom," Daisy said, hands on her hips, "butt out."

Rita never lost stride. She tossed her purse onto the passenger seat, climbed into the car, and pretended her daughter wasn't glaring at her. "You two belong together, Daisy. It would make me very upset if you two didn't stay together because of something as simple as living arrangements. Lots of couples don't live in the same house. Just think of it as a way to keep love new."

Daisy knew all that; she just didn't think her mother should be so pushy. "We're happy the way things are going."

Unperturbed by her daughter's warning tone and look that said "Mind your own business,"

Rita blew her a kiss and turned the key in the ignition. "Love you, too. Ta, ta."

Daisy rolled her eyes and blew a kiss back to her mother. She watched as Rita cut a hard U-turn on the gravel, spun out, then zoomed down the highway as if the speed limit was seventy instead of fifty.

Back in the house, Daisy said, "You don't have to do this, Kenneth." She was embarrassed that he'd been put in a tough predicament.

Kenneth pulled her into his arms and kissed her on the top of her head. "Your mother has too much class to send me out to check on a ramshackle house. We both know this already, so lighten up. Besides, I'm curious."

Daisy squeezed him around the middle. "Me, too, I have to admit. I find it interesting the house is available for rent or sale, which keeps your options open."

"Yeah," Kenneth said, his face thoughtful as they returned to their seats at the kitchen table. He'd rinsed the dishes while the women were saying good-bye. "The fact the joint is vacant is what interests me."

"I noticed."

"Know which house it is?"

Daisy threw up her hands in an I-give-up gesture. "Nope. I do know that if you aren't careful, Mom will have you living in that house tomorrow morning and the place furnished by Rent-A-Center before tomorrow night."

Kenneth laughed. He had been in Guthrie enough times to be familiar with the location of major businesses in town. Rent-A-Center was sandwiched between Dollar General and Mega Movies in a convenience strip mall on South Division. "She'll have it accessorized with Wally World decor."

"Mmm-hmm," Daisy said. "She'll have everything from towels and bedding to bread for the refrigerator and plates for the kitchen cupboards. Anyway, let's get back to Kandi Kane and her daughter, Sugar."

"Go ahead."

"Kandi is a journalist who specializes in the gardening circuit niche. Sugar is her daughter and publicist."

Kenneth tapped a finger on the tabletop twice and then stopped. "The way you say the girl's name makes it sound like she's trouble."

"Sugar tries to be sweet but she really isn't," Daisy said. There was no use trying to be diplomatic. He'd find out anyway.

Kenneth thought about the elderly women he'd run into at Gus' Liquor Store, Miss Myrtle and Miss Tilly. They'd been jazzed, excited about possible fireworks at the garden show. "I'm concerned about all the hotheads."

Daisy sighed hard and rose from the table. "Wait until you meet Kandi. She ought to be here any minute."

A beautiful new Chrysler sedan covered the road at forty miles per hour, ten miles under the posted speed limit on Highway 77 going north toward the center of Guthrie. Kandi Kane checked her lipstick in the rearview mirror, then blew a kiss at her reflection because she looked too damned good in her Velvet Crush lipstick by Maybelline, with its coordinated shades of blush and eye shadow.

Feeling as if she looked good gave her confidence, but being in Guthrie for the garden show brought out the nasty in her. She had an ax to grind in Guthrie, people to see, to get even with, and the garden show was perfect cover. People had expected her to be rude but they didn't expect her to be rude with an agenda.

She'd been edgy in Wal-Mart, which had done nothing for her private nerves or her public image. Small towns reminded her of the low-key hometown where she'd been raised, and she hated to think of home.

There was no way in the world she'd ever live in a small town again—ever—but no matter how hard she tried to pretend otherwise, Kandi was a small-town girl at heart, a Nebraska farm girl. She'd traveled all over the United States, and despite all the wonderful sights she'd seen, she best enjoyed the open spaces found in rural America, the wildflowers and wild animals, pastures full of goats or sheep or horses or cows. She liked a good thunderstorm, the sound of cicadas at night, the music wind made as it blew through trees and tall grasses, the sight of bright stars in the sky, the clean air and sense of unspoiled innocence that people from large industrial cities called country.

She'd discovered early in her career that life could be a bitch, something she believed in after she divorced her husband. She hadn't lived in a small town since, nor had she ever married again. She thought marriage was for suckers.

Kandi's best asset from her marriage was the creation of her only child, Sugar, a young woman who had grown into someone both bitter and sweet, like a chocolate best suited for baking instead of eating right out of a silver foil wrapper, Hershey's Kisses-style. She spoke to her reflection. "Today, we're gonna get even."

At the sight of the sign saying DAISY'S ROSE NURSERY AND GARDEN SHOP, she flashed her signal to turn right. The property was composed of rustic and weathered buildings surrounded by gardens so lavish it was hard for Kandi to believe most everything was for sale or that she was in farm country.

Daisy's roses were not squashed together; they were grouped by color and laid out in half-crescent shapes with a walking path for customers to use while browsing.

The business was separated from the house by a grove of redbud trees and a deep green lawn. There was a privacy hedge composed of Siberian elm kept trimmed to roughly twelve feet. On the south side of the elm fence was the business; on the north side was Daisy's personal residence.

To the untrained eye, Daisy's private garden

was a continuation of the nursery and garden shop, but to Kandi's professional eye, there was an exquisite sense of order about the garden that made Kandi, despite her garden expertise, feel welcome and pleased. Daisy's private gardens enticed the senses and soul, so that when Kandi pulled into the drive she sighed with relief.

Her car, with its glossy surface and sleek lines, looked out of place next to Daisy's dusty work truck with its load of decorative red native sandstone in the back. Idly, Kandi wondered if the stone would be used in Daisy's home or in her business. For the first time in a long time, Kandi felt like getting her hands dirty with actual yard work.

It had been a long time since she'd worn a pair of faded jeans and rubber gardening boots. It was 12:00 P.M., high noon. The sun was so hot, Kandi felt as if its heat was melting all the tension from her body.

There was no breeze, and yet the presence of Daisy's gardens had the effect of cool running water. Lush green foliage, vibrant reds and purples and pinks in flowers so strong and beautiful Kandi felt a surprise surge of delight and anticipation that she would be a key factor in Daisy Rogers's first garden show, but when Kandi remembered her true reason for accepting the invitation to attend the exhibition, a shadow darkened her features and brought a scowl to her face.

Daisy opened her front door and was not surprised to see the ugly look on Kandi's face. The woman was always scowling, always dissatisfied about something, if what was said in the press was true. Daisy threw an extra watt into her smile. "It's great to see you, Kandi. Come on in."

Kandi really wanted a tour of the gardens. Her tone was arrogant even though she didn't mean to be rude. "Where exactly will the exhibition take place?" She hadn't meant to skip the small talk, either, and realized how poorly she presented herself to her casually dressed hostess.

Daisy hadn't expected any other type of behavior. She didn't mind sticking to business. "At the fairgrounds." Her tone was cordial.

"On Division?"

"Yes."

"It's amazing how much I remember about this place," Kandi said as her eyes searched the quiet. "Haven't been here since my daughter graduated from Langston two years ago."

"There's been a lot of changes in town since then."

Kandi's laugh was genuine and surprised them both. "I saw some of them, like the Fleetwood homes on Industrial and Division, the new storage place next to Roller World. By the way, I can't believe the roller rink is really a bingo parlor. Why can't the bingo people get their own place around here?"

"Good question," Daisy said, her brows tilted

at a how-should-I-know angle. "Would you like me to show you around the gardens?"

"Please."

Kandi looked as relieved as she felt. This was one occasion when she would enjoy the behind-the-scenes activities associated with being a keynote speaker at a public gardening event. In a larger city, they might have met in a restaurant to run over the details of the show, but in this small-town arena, the professional edge was less cutthroat and more humanity based.

In this instance, Kandi knew she was being treated to a rare insider's view of Daisy's passion for gardening. The experience was similar to a bookworm visiting another bookworm's private library. When Kandi spoke, her gratitude and pleasure were genuine. "I'd like that. Thank you."

"You're welcome."

Kandi was older than Daisy by twenty-two years but she looked every bit as healthy and alive as Daisy did. The most significant contrast between them stemmed from the aura they presented.

Kandi was serious, forceful, dynamic in her beauty. She was five feet six inches tall, carried her weight well, looked as if she exercised on a regular basis. She was manicured, from her hair to the French pedicure on her clipped and pampered toes.

Her clothes were loose and free on her body, the tropical colored fabric lightweight and as obviously expensive as the understated perfume she wore and the close-cropped precision cut on her head.

Daisy was open, friendly, charismatic, a universally attractive woman, universal because she appealed equally to men and women, both sexes drawn to her easygoing manner. Her dress reflected her present state of mind.

She wore navy capri pants with a pale green tank top, a straw hat and green gardening clogs. The image she presented was one of a young woman strolling through a meadow with a basket of fresh-cut flowers carried in the crook of one arm as she made her way to the potting shed in order to arrange them.

The women crossed the gravel on the ground in front of Daisy's house and met Kenneth partway in his approach. A healthy man in his physical prime, he looked as if he didn't have a care in the world, as if his entire being was centered and his future was not only known but on track, his master-life design the perfect complement to his personality.

Kandi was astute enough to notice that Kenneth's self-assuredness matched Daisy's composure in parallel lines and that together they made a formidable couple. She admired their obvious rightness and unity together.

On the short walk to Daisy's front door, Kandi cataloged the minutiae of her immediate view: the slate color of the gravel, the tenacity of volunteer elm trees growing between cobbled flagstones.

She noticed a crumbly dirt mixture and knew

immediately that the mound she saw was the final stage of a compost pile. The compost was situated next to a roughly four-foot-tall green-house made of glass. Inside the glass structure were assorted plants in small pots, mostly seedlings and herbs.

Again, Kandi had the urge to throw on some jeans and rubber gardening shoes in order to explore the visual treats in Daisy's gardens. They were as friendly and inviting as the woman who'd created them.

With effort, Kandi reminded herself of the true purpose she had in accepting Daisy's invitation: revenge. It was too bad Daisy and her lover would play a part in her own personal drama. Kandi shrugged once more. As far as she was concerned, casualties existed in every war, especially those between friends and business relationships.

Inside the house, she noticed the German shepherd. "Big dog you've got there." She said it with the cautious respect a large dog generates in people who don't know it. The dog flicked her tail twice but made no move to sniff or otherwise investigate Kandi.

Daisy eyed her seventy-five-pound canine with affection. "Her name is Cutie Pie." Quiet in general, loyal as a rule, the German shepherd was Daisy's secret weapon. If the dog ever thought her owner was in danger, she switched from friendly calm to deadly adversary in less time than it took to blink.

Kandi snorted in disbelief. "If you say so."

In her book, Cutie Pie was a fit name for a toy poodle. This dog had the regal bearing of a queen and the watchful gaze of a trained soldier. With the shepherd around, Kandi doubted anyone would get ideas about raiding Daisy's home while she was working in the garden shop. Cutie Pie had the power and mind-set to chew up a trespasser and leave him for Daisy to find in the driveway. Kenneth Gunn and Cutie Pie made excellent protectors.

Kandi felt a stab of envy. This was one of those odd occasions when she wished she'd chosen a more traditional path for herself. She had a gorgeous home, a carefully constructed career, but she lacked true quality in her private life, such as treasured friends and other gratifying relationships.

In Daisy's kitchen, cream Formica counters were adorned with white appliances, and clearly, the most commonly used appliance of all was the twelve-cup coffeepot, currently filled with fresh brew. The white theme brought to mind a cleanness and purity of spirit that served to make Daisy's home a nonthreatening place to be. Kandi was struck by the wholesome, balanced part of her hostess's creative spirit. To drink coffee in this setting was like drinking happiness from the bowl of a clean ceramic cup in an open room filled with the soothing light of friendship.

Beside the coffeepot was a stainless-steel coffee grinder and several clear jars of whole coffee beans. The labels on the jars read

"Henry's," "Post Alley Decaf," "Taza Doro Espresso" and "Seattle's Best." "I love this coffee," she said, her eyes lit up.

"Me, too," Daisy said. "I get it right here in
town."

Daisy's come-what-may attitude soothed Kenneth as much as it did Kandi who sat at the
kitchen table with her shoes kicked off and her
nose held over the steam rising from the cup
she held in her manicured hands.

Kenneth understood Kandi's immediate sense
of welcome and relaxation because he'd felt the
same way when he first sat at Daisy's table. Then,
he'd been physically injured and suffering from
amnesia. Her no-nonsense attitude, reflected in
her kitchen decor, had helped him deal with the
pain and suffering he experienced over being
beaten and left for dead on her property.

Daisy's nails weren't polished like Kandi's—
they were chipped on two fingers—and yet it
was from those caring hands that the wonderful, fresh ground coffee was made, as was the
lush garden view from the windows in her quiet
kitchen, the sound of birds outside serving as
background music.

For the second time since waking up with
Daisy that morning, Kenneth felt blessed to be
a part of her life. Her mother's suggestion to
relocate to Guthrie for good was very appealing,
especially during nearly spiritual, entirely uplifting moments like these.

As Daisy and Kandi discussed the flower show,
he allowed himself to fully unwind, his mind

registering the even rhythm of Daisy's words the way he might assimilate the sound of some type of healing music, the sound of wind or sea during moments of calm.

Kandi's presence was the only discordant note in the bucolic setting. Kandi, with her sleek car and her chic look and her history of nastiness and aggression. Those were not qualities found in Daisy's basic personality or her living environment.

There was an odd sort of quiet going on as they all shared coffee together. It was, for Kenneth, much like riding on an airplane with strangers who were content to be silent, people who were not compelled to talk to neighbors in order to pass time. Instead they slept or read or meditated, eyes focused casually into space.

Almost idly, Kenneth glanced at Kandi Kane and wondered if she would prove to be the storm after all the calm in Daisy's kitchen. He pushed away the thought, focused on nothing particular, his eyes touching everything around him as he evaluated the decision to move to Guthrie in order to be near Daisy full-time.

Like Kandi did, he thought her kitchen was descriptive of her style of living. The kitchen was highly efficient, with little clutter. The center cooking island and convenience sink were as neat as the countertops. Cookbooks were lined up beside books on growing herbs and making skincare products from the bounty of her tiny kitchen garden.

There were small pots of living plants, nothing fancy, but the fact the greenery was healthy and thriving showed Daisy's care for the simplest aspects of gardening as much as she did the larger ones, like growing companion plants to sell with the roses in her commercial gardens. The Russell lupines in purples and blues had become his favorites.

"Hey," Daisy said, "Kenneth?"

He laughed a little self-consciously. "Daydreaming."

Kandi eyed him with open speculation. "Some private eye you are. I thought you all were edgy, cigarette-smoking, whiskey-drinking, live-on-the-edge kind of guys. You look like a corporate dot com exec of some type."

Kenneth appraised Kandi just as coldly, but unlike her, his tone was neither here nor there, it was entirely neutral. "Don't bite your tongue."

It was obvious to Daisy, Kandi wasn't sure if she'd been insulted or invited to further speak her mind. She decided to take control of the conversation by putting an end to it. "Kandi, I'm sure you're tired and will want to rest at your hotel. Call me in the morning and we'll get together for lunch."

Kandi gave her a give-me-a-break look. "Don't try to manipulate me. I'll go when I'm good and ready."

This, Kenneth decided, was the Kandi that Daisy had warned him about. He wrestled Kandi's attention away from their hostess. "I'll walk you to your car."

Kandi seldom argued with handsome men,

especially young handsome men like Kenneth.
Tension fell away from her face with the ease
of a seasoned actress, which is exactly what she
was being at that particular moment. Her problem was that she didn't feel like driving all the
way to Edmond after winding down at Daisy's.

If she'd known she'd be this at ease after her
meeting, she would have stayed at Amy's Place
on the corner of Vilas and First Street, just
three miles away from Daisy's house, instead of
driving the twenty miles to the Ramada Inn.
Amy's Place, a bed-and-breakfast that specialized in everything from facials to full-body massage and reflexology, would have been the
perfect way to cap off the last hour she'd spent
with Daisy and Kenneth.

"You're right," she said. "I am tired." She
gathered her purse and shoved her feet back
into shoes that were so tight they made her toes
hurt. Still, despite her snippy remarks, Kandi
had made herself a much-sought-after commod-
ity by being all vinegar and a little salt. Salt was
a natural preservative.

She used just enough salt in her conversation
to guarantee a listener's attention but not so
much salt she repeatedly spoiled public taste for
the words she cooked up in her syndicated writing column on gardening. There was never a
viable substitute for honest and true good man-
ners. She used them to say, "Thanks for the
coffee and the tour."

Those were the last kind words she'd ever
have to say to anyone.

Four

That evening, around 8:00 o'clock, Daisy was so tired she could hardly stand up straight. She'd been sharing the lifting, hauling, and arranging chores with Kenneth at the fairgrounds. The couple now sat at a bistro table in the shade garden on the east side of the house, a pad of plain white paper and a pencil between them.

On the 8 1/2 x 11 inch ruled paper, they roughed out the final design of the show, based on the placement of the items they'd just moved, which was basically table and chairs and trash receptacles. The paper read:

A		K		Hospitality
B	D	L	Books	
C	E F	M		
	G H		Garden	Classes and
	I J		Accessories	Demonstrations

Each letter represented an exhibit. Elena's Bookstore would be there to sell related plant and landscape books that were specific to Oklahoma gardening. Rose and Dwayne Garden Accessories would supply gardening knickknacks ranging from wind chimes to citronella candles

to garden-specific apparel to unique yard ornaments such as gazing balls and decorative rain
gauges and wall thermometers.

They specialized in the selling of starter garden kits for people interested in attracting mon-
archs and gave pointers on how to safely repel
garden pests such as deer and gophers. Both
businesses sent customers her way and in turn,
Daisy did the same for them.

Miss Tilly and Miss Myrtle were handling this
part of the show exclusively for Daisy. Both
women were great friends with Rita Rogers and
both women were charter members of Daisy's
garden club.

Without the solid support of these retired
women, Daisy knew she wouldn't have approached such a large venture with such confidence. The garden club members, charter
members in particular, were as compelled as she
was to make this event a much-celebrated and
talked-about one. Excitement was contagious
and high, much like the harried days before a
wedding ceremony.

Daisy used a finger to push her bangs away
from a brow that glistened with sweat from the
heat of the sun and from exerting herself at the
fairgrounds. "Kenneth," she said, "I'm so glad
you're here to help me get through all this
stuff."

"So am I."

She sighed, temporarily overwhelmed by the
many things she had left to do. "All the details
are driving me nuts. Everybody who wants to

enter a class or specimen for show has to have a schedule prior to the event. The deadlines for early and regular registration have to be met, which means that entry blanks have to be checked for completion and then processed. Ya da, ya da, ya da."

She also had to be sure that guidelines were sent to all the approved registrants. She'd printed up information on how to cut and condition specimens for show, how to transport them to the show, and what limitations were required for displaying the specimens, such as how much primping could be done. For example, pesticide or bug damage was okay to remove but no cosmetic changes such as wiring, oiling, or coloring would be permitted. Doing so would disqualify an exhibitor's entry into the show.

All of the exhibits had to be clearly labeled by name and class on plastic labels with permanent black fine-point marking pens. This would ensure a uniform look to every physical exhibit. Daisy was a firm believer that details would make the difference between an average showing and an excellent showing, which meant the less guesswork involved in the exhibition the better, an ideal that went for judging as well as showing.

Kenneth stood from his chair, moved to stand behind Daisy, and put his hands on her shoulders. Her muscles were so tense, he opted to knead her neck and shoulder area in order to help her relax.

He felt her groan of pure pleasure right down to his toes. He even released her hair from its ponytail and massaged her scalp. Her hair was soft and healthy, its strands coated with a mildly scented herbal oil for sheen and to reduce dryness. He liked the weight and texture of it between his fingertips.

Daisy wasn't long on make-up but she was faithful about using quality skin- and hair-care products. As a result of her regular regimen, Kenneth found himself stroking her skin and smelling her hair as often as time permitted. There was never enough time to do all he wanted for as long as he wanted, but for now Kenneth intended to fully savor the moment.

When she threw her head back and purred, it was all he could do not to make love to her on the spot, right there between her collection of orange, yellow, and red roses that smelled of heaven.

He stilled himself, carefully, so that he allowed his full senses to linger over the woman and the moment. For Kenneth, lingering on the subtleties of Daisy's moods was a sensual prelude to the love they would make together during the night. The anticipation he felt was exquisite.

"Take care of all the details you need to take care of," he said. "Leave the big things to me. The last of the props, the hauling and lifting and shoving around that needs to be done. Use this paper to draw diagrams of what you want regarding placement. As far as set-up goes, save yourself for the fine-tuning and leave the rest to me." She had insisted on helping earlier and he had agreed, against his best judgment, in order to make her happy. He had no desire to see her this physically exhausted again.

Daisy stopped the massage by gripping his wrists with her hands. He felt strong and competent, the force of his hands tempered to soothe and calm her frazzled nerves. Just being near him made her feel good. "I feel really fortunate to have a guy like you."

Kenneth resumed his seat, his legs spread out in front of him, his shoes kicked off, his toes wiggling in the cool dark grass surrounding the flowers in Daisy's garden. The sound of cicadas was loud in his ears. "What do you mean?"

She was glad to explain. "Instead of moaning and groaning because my schedule is too hectic for me to snuggle with you half the day, you aren't giving me a hard time. You're being supportive and I really need that right now."

"Complaining won't do anything but build a wall between us. We live too far away from each other to build another barrier. As long as we spend our nights together, the rest will work itself out. I haven't given up any of my dreams or goals and it isn't fair for me to ask you to do it. It's our differences that make us special anyway."

Daisy scooted her chair closer to his, kicked off her rubber clogs, and played footsie. Next to hers, Kenneth's feet were huge, wide, his smaller toes crooked and callused from the basketball shoes he favored. "I've done a lot of thinking about the house hunting Mom's been plotting for you. It would be great if we lived in the same city."

"I agree. To be honest, I'm really considering it. I wouldn't give up my career, though." He enjoyed his work too much to let it go completely. He just needed to be creative in choosing a line of work that was comparable and equally rewarding.

Daisy had never stopped being aware of Kenneth's work-related dilemmas. She believed it was a deeply personal issue he needed to resolve for himself. That way his final decisions would be his own. "If you move your agency, you'd lose more than half your clients, wouldn't you?"

"I talked to Spud Gurber about possible work in this area. He suggested that I contact one of his friends at UPS about investigating collisions involving delivery drivers. This might include workmen's comp claims." Spud Gurber was a Guthrie police officer.

"You're kidding?"

"No."

Daisy couldn't believe what she was hearing just then. On the one hand, she was definitely thrilled Kenneth had a solid lead on an alternative career. On the other hand, she was shocked to discover she wasn't the only person in Guthrie he was building a steady relationship with. It was a definite sign he was laying the groundwork for a new home base. "When did you talk to Spud?" She and Spud had grown up together.

Almost detached, Kenneth assessed her reaction. He'd wanted her to understand that she was a factor in his decision-making process, but not the only one. For him, moving to Guthrie was no longer an abstract idea fueled by the sexual desire he felt for Daisy. "I called Spud from Wichita about two weeks before I flew out here."

"I didn't realize you two kept in such close contact with each other."

"He's level-headed and fair," Kenneth explained. He was glad she wasn't truly miffed that he hadn't kept her apprised of the Guthrie contacts he'd maintained after he first met her. His relationship with Daisy was personal.

His relationship with Spud was largely professional and he had no problem keeping the two separate. It was clear to Kenneth that Daisy recognized and appreciated the subtle difference; she didn't question him about his choice of confidant. Her expression was open, her eyes attentive.

He said, "I trust his judgment. When I let him know I was thinking about relocating to Guthrie, he said he'd put some feelers out about work opportunities."

Daisy smiled. "That explains why you took my mother's suggestions about house hunting so seriously. You were already thinking of coming to Guthrie."

"Yes. I can't see myself crafting yard ornaments full-time for a living, and even if I could do it, the shift in lifestyle would be too dramatic for me. I don't think I'm equipped to go cold turkey. I like my work too much to quit now."

"I understand. It's why I don't drop everything to move to Wichita. Some of my women friends think I'm crazy not to marry you, and that long-distance relationships don't work. Too many distractions."

"News flash, Daisy. This long-distance thing isn't working. Not for me, anyway. I don't see you enough." He felt as if he'd said that a million times and still she pretended not to hear him, still refused to acknowledge his point.

A defensive wall shuttered her eyes. "But it makes the coming together again so much sweeter."

"I need more stability than that."

She stilled her thudding heart by taking deep yoga breaths. They'd both had a long day. "I don't want to fight with you, Kenneth."

He refused to drop the subject, what he considered a critical one between them. "Every time I want to get closer to you, you run away. Why?"

"My independence is important to me. Most of my friends married the loves of their lives to immediately be taken advantage of by husbands who are suddenly too busy to care about the details."

"What are you talking about?"

"I'm talking about flowers and candy and long drives and banana splits just because. I'm talking about holding hands and cracking jokes and frittering away the day doing nothing spectacular beyond being held in each other's arms. We have that all the time now, but if we were to live in the same house together, it would all stop. We'd get hung up on the day-to-day grind and I'm not going down like that, even if it means growing old alone."

He considered this point of view self-destructive. Many marriages in the Guthrie area exceeded the half-century mark, something he saw whenever he read the *Guthrie News Leader* newspaper. Kenneth felt there was nothing in their mutual chemistry that indicated, at least to him, that their union was destined to be short-lived. He said with disgust, "You sound like marriage is a death sentence."

She didn't have to think about a response. It came quick, her words clipped and edged with heat. "I like my freedom. I like knowing my bills and car and house are paid off. I even own my business outright. I can pick up and go anywhere I want anytime I want. Nobody second-guesses me."

Kenneth forced his aggression in check. "You're really off on a tangent here. I don't understand why you're so pissed or why you think I'd want to own you as if you were a piece of property. Everything you just said cuts both ways."

Daisy wanted him to see where she was coming from. "It's just that I've seen my closest women friends slowly become disillusioned with

life. They stop polishing their toes and fingernails and wearing make-up on a regular basis.
They don't dress up anymore unless it's for a
special event."

Before she could finish speaking, he was already shaking his head no. "That's superficial
and could easily be labeled lazy behavior. Some
women gain weight and get sloppy with their
appearance because they've hooked a man and
married him or had kids by him or found some
other way to hang on to him and claim exclusivity rights. It really bothers me that you think
so little of me. There are good relationships out
there and you have to know about some of
them yourself."

Daisy sighed. She knew she wasn't being reasonable. Still, her feelings were honest and true.
"I do."

"Then why are you expecting the worst-case
scenario for us? Why are you predicting failure?"

She recognized that he felt she was being self-
absorbed and emotional. He wasn't interested
in being a salve to her occasional bout of loneliness. He wanted more from her and he deserved to get it. She simply didn't want to
superimpose his needs and wants over hers, especially at the start of their love affair.

With controlled emotion, she broke the heavy
silence between them. "As bad as I might like
it, I don't want you to relocate and get mad at
me later because you aren't happy. Guthrie
might not be much to some people but it's

home to me. I don't want you to spoil things for me if you decide later that you've made a mistake. My friends are here. My family is here. My life is here."

Kenneth was capable of observing reality and making adjustments to it that achieved whatever goal he wanted. What he wanted was Daisy. Force would only run her away from him. Still, his feelings were as real as her own. "Do you love me for myself or for the thrill of a distant lover?"

"Both."

His eyes snapped over her emotions like a whip, harsh and without mercy. "Not good enough."

She snapped right back, with a stinging bitterness that reflected the attitude that went with her words. "Take it or leave it."

God, he loved her, and, man, was he pissed off. "Look, Daisy. I know you're stressed-out about this flower show and tripping because this Kandi Kane is a real piece of work, but don't take the good thing we have together and push it away. Don't get us to the point where we start issuing ultimatums to each other.

"I could say marry me or I'll leave, but I'm not doing that. I'm not demanding you give up anything you've earned, especially your privacy, but you can't treat me like a stray that may or may not stay in your life. I'm a man and real men stand up for what they believe in. I believe in you, I believe in us.

"I believe we have a serious future together,

but I'm not going to beg you for a chance to be in your life. I can leave right now and we'd both be miserable and we'd both find a way to move forward, but that's not what I want and that's not a safety net I'm looking to hold together. Love isn't safe and it isn't blind and it isn't always fun, but it's still a good thing. It's worth fighting for. You are worth fighting for, but I do have my pride and I'm too proud to beg. I'd rather starve than ask you for a bone when I know you don't want to give it."

Head cocked to the side, she eyed him as she would an empty but usable space in her garden. "You'd actually move here and be happy?"

He looked at her as if she was a witness entangled between the harsh edge of truth and the comfort of a self-deluding lie. He wanted no lies to thrive between them. "I was thinking about relocating before I ever laid eyes on you, Daisy. As you very well remember, I was out here working on a lead in a murder investigation. I liked Guthrie then. I've come to really enjoy it, largely because you're here, but also because of the potential it has for growth and my own chance to follow my dreams."

"Which are?"

He didn't have to spend three seconds thinking up a response. He thought about it constantly. Any major change in lifestyle deserved study from all angles. "To own my own land. To do carpentry work. To retire in peace on my own property. To fish when I feel like it and be bothered with people when I feel like it. To look out my window and not see another house twenty feet away. I want a dog or two.

"I don't plan on being a private detective for the rest of my life, but I do intend to use my training to help me gain and maintain the lifestyle I see for myself. You are part of that vision, Daisy, but I don't believe in force and I won't be forcing myself or my plans on you. You either want to be with me or you don't. Make up your mind one way or the other."

Her voice and face held a look of warning. "Don't make me choose."

Kenneth exploded, coldly, every word producing heat loss in Daisy's own anger. He'd never been this angry with her before. Ever. "What in the world are you talking about, Daisy? Choose? Choose what? We're a couple, aren't we?"

Daisy's pulse felt arrested. Time stopped. This was a turning point for them—explosive, life altering, imperative. She said, softly, "Yes." Her paranoia about the future was one thing, but her love for Kenneth was clear in her mind.

"Then there is no choice," he stated flatly. "It's a continuation. You can't have a rose without the basics as in sun, soil, and water. You can't have a relationship without the basics, either, as in trust, faith, and fidelity. I believe in you as my lover and as my friend. If that's not enough for you, nothing will ever be and we might as well end this thing now because a thing is all it is."

Daisy's heart said, *Girl, this is it.* Her mouth said, "Don't go."

Kenneth laid all his cards on the table. He had a lot to lose by not speaking his mind. "Don't make me go by creating a lot of bull when there doesn't have to be any. I'm not asking you to give up anything more than you're asking of me. It's not fifty-fifty, but what we have is close enough that percentages don't matter to me."

Her lip had a slight curl to it. Her eyes hit him with a quick one-two, one-two. "What do you mean we're not fifty-fifty?"

Kenneth glared at her. "I'm spending my vacation time and my money to visit you on a regular basis. In return, I expect exclusivity as in no other man in your life. I expect to spend as much time with you as possible before I have to leave for Wichita again. I don't care if we spend that time in restaurants or your business or your home. I just want to be with you, Daisy. Why? Because I love you. When I'm coming down here on my own dime in exchange for whatever time you have available, I'm giving more than fifty percent."

Daisy pressed her lips together. Tight.

Kenneth wanted to hear whatever it was she was having a hard time controlling. "What part of what I said is making you want to cuss me out?"

"I don't like the idea that you think you're giving more than you're receiving."

Kenneth laughed, but there wasn't any humor in his voice. "I'm getting what I want, Daisy, just not enough of it. I don't mind tooling around your garden shop because it's not an all-day thing and I actually find it restful. But the only reason I'm in your space is because of you. Everything else going on is extra. I'm not ready to retire and I have no intention of being your flunky."

"Flunky?"

Kenneth almost didn't respond to the question. He'd never seen her look so mean. She was so mad she could hardly breathe. Her chest heaved, her nose flared, her hands were clenched.

"Absolutely," he said. "I'm hauling and lifting and building and whatever else because making you happy makes me happy. We get the chance to work together without cramping each other's style or usurping each other's authority in any way. You don't know squat about building gazebos and I don't know jack about roses but the two go together."

Daisy blew off a long breath before she said, "Okay. What you're saying is true. I've just got a phobia or something about my independence."

Kenneth nodded sagely, as if he had an idea of what she might say next. He didn't. He was just glad she preferred talking to kicking him off her property and out of her life. "Your independence is part of what makes you special to me. I'm too old not to know what I want and how to take care of it when I get it."

She flexed her fist against the tabletop. "I'm not an it."

His voice was hoarse. "Who burned you?"

She pressed her lips together again.

"Obviously," he said, "we can't go any further with this relationship unless we figure out what your wall is all about. Do you even know?"

"My wall?"

"Yes."

"Before my parents split up, I remember my mom cried a lot."

"Did your dad hit her?"

"No. I think she was crying because she wanted to hold the family together but didn't see how she could do it without him pitching in."

"As in helping around the house and all that?"

"No. Emotionally. Dad did all the right things about fidelity and responsibility but he kept himself to himself. He loved us, but he loved himself more. I remember hearing him say once that he just wanted to make himself happy."

"That's bull."

"I figured Mom thought the same thing. She left him but I think she always believed he wouldn't let her go. He did."

"Did he ever remarry?"

"No."

"Maybe he wasn't the marrying kind."

"Some men aren't and I believe he knew that," Daisy said. "Mom thought she could love him enough to fill in the gaps that were missing in their marriage but she couldn't. It takes two to make a couple and two to make it work. I think the harder Mom tried the more Dad ran for cover. If it hadn't been for children, they probably wouldn't have lasted as long as they had. I find it interesting that neither of them married again although they both dated."

Kenneth tried to make sense of Daisy's ramble. "Okay. What you're telling me is that you think you're like your dad in that you don't want to commit."

"Yes. I know I don't want marriage or children or a live-in lover. A lot of people in town think I'm strange because I'm not married."

"That's ridiculous."

"It is, but I think there are still negative stereotypes in our society about women who choose not to marry. Personally, I think it's simpler to stay single."

Kenneth took her hands within his own. "Listen. We can still grow old together. I've been single my whole life. It's the committed relationship with you that I'm after. There are a number of couples who are married but live in separate parts of the house, couples who live in separate homes but visit when it suits them, couples who marry and never have children. As long as you and I are happy, nothing else matters. If we decide to split up, there won't be any property to divide or children to worry over. Why don't we just put all this stuff behind us once and for all?"

Daisy felt as if a huge burden had been lifted off her shoulders. She really hoped he meant what he was saying. "Okay. Sounds good to me. To tell you the truth, I'm glad we got all that out. Does this mean you're seriously considering moving here?"

"There are advantages. I can own a property outright for the airfare I'm spending. It isn't practical to keep doing things the way we are and we both know it. Long-distance love isn't just about romance. It's about finance."

She made a face at him. "Why are you talking about money so much?"

"Because it matters. I've got bills and a condo and a lifestyle to satisfy. If I was broke and toothless and begging for cash you wouldn't have anything to do with me. I've got plenty of disposable income, a sound investment program, a lucrative business, and a full life ahead of me. I want to visit every capital city in the United States and then travel to Europe. I'd love to do those things with you. Call me old-fashioned, but I still believe in providing for the woman I love the things that are in my power to give. Time and money are the two top ways I believe a man can romance the woman he loves.

"It takes cash to court a woman and cash to keep her," he said. "I also need to work for my own sanity and self-worth. Same as you. I'm talking about money because it's a critical issue for a self-employed man moving from a big city to a small town. The kind of work a man does, and the kind of woman he calls his own, are major yardsticks to use when measuring a man's worth. I'm not willing to throw away a great career or a great woman."

She eyed him carefully. "You've thought this through."

"I have."

"When's your target date for moving?"

"My condo is on the market," he said. "I've got a couple of pretty promising nibbles through a real estate agent friend."

Daisy asked the one question she'd been burning to ask when she found out Kenneth had been keeping up a friendship with Spud Gurber. "Did my mother know? Is that why she's been running all over the place looking for property you might like to buy?"

"Coincidental. It's my conversation with Spud that let me know I could swing it with the right connections. Your mom has known me long enough to have a strong idea about what I'd like in a home. She just wants to help us stay together."

Daisy smiled. "I think we've covered every base, don't you?"

Kenneth said, "Almost." He pulled her onto his lap and pressed his lips to hers. The kiss was slow and meaningful, profound in that it sealed their unity as neatly as any proper kiss in a proper wedding.

From his pocket, Kenneth extracted a jewelry box. Inside the box was an amethyst ring, its band made of gold, its jewel shaped like a heart. Amethyst was Daisy's birthstone.

He said, "This might work and it might not
work, but this birthstone is yours to keep. Dia-
monds aren't always forever. Your birthstone
is."

She opened her mouth to speak but before
she could get a word out, he shushed her with
a long finger over her lips. "You belong to me,
Daisy, and this ring is a symbol of my commitment to making this relationship work."

Unable to think of words to say that showed
the exact nature of her feelings just then, Daisy
took Kenneth by the hand and headed toward
the house. "Come on," she said. "I've got a
claim to stake myself."

He laughed. "This day couldn't get any better."

Five

It was the next day—Tuesday. Stella Fitzgerald didn't think life could get much better. A local Guthrie journalist for a small independent paper, she had the unfortunate habit of getting her facts mixed up with the fiction she tended to report in her gardening column.

She'd always longed to publish a book, but books took too long to write and short stories were harder to pull off than she'd thought when she first decided to satisfy her itch to write. She found it difficult to sit down for longer than an hour, which was about how long it took for her to write a draft of a newspaper article.

Stella was convinced that the secret to her gardening success, aside from constant conditioning to the clay soil particular to Guthrie, was to sing to her plants. She believed that all living things benefited from the gift of song.

Regardless of what others might say of her strategy for successful gardening, everyone was in agreement that Stella's garden, a three-hundred-foot double-border flower bed, was a treat to the eye, almost year-round.

She lived in a single-story, A-frame house, with one bedroom, one bath, a living room, and a kitchen. The house, brick red with charcoal-gray trim, was perfectly offset with the most beautiful garden on the stretch of Drexel Avenue between Harrison and Oklahoma Streets where she lived.

On this particular day, Stella sang to her plants, as she methodically set about pinching off the spent blooms of her bachelor's buttons, and Mexican sunflowers and pinwheel zinnias. Across the street from her stood the Scottish Rite Temple, a building originally designed to house the state capitol of Oklahoma.

Its graceful lines were a peaceful view from Stella's front gardens, but it was the wide expanse of green lawn that formed the perfect backdrop to her profusion of colorful plants, a collection that didn't have a single rose in the bunch, a marvel that Daisy often laughed about on the rare occasions she visited Stella's home.

Thinking of Daisy, working in her garden, enjoying life, anticipating the imminent arrival of Kandi Kane and possibly her daughter, Sugar, caused Stella to burst into song so loud that the hummingbirds jetted away from the purple budelia bush and joggers paused to look her way in surprise.

Stella didn't care about how she looked or what other people thought about what she did in her own front yard. She was forty-eight years old, reasonably fit, though she was a little more jiggly under the arms and neck than she wanted to be.

She enjoyed studying and reporting on special-interest groups, such as enthusiasts at Daisy's upcoming garden show, then choosing select people within the group to analyze and report about in the articles she published. It was this sort of observation and analysis that uncovered dirt on Kandi Kane.

Stella was ready to get noticed, not as an eccentric, self-trained gardening journalist, but as a superb analyst of the Guthrie social scene. She hoped Daisy's garden show would help her gain the type of attention she craved. Thinking of writing reminded her of Daisy's impending visit to run over the basic outline and schedule of the garden show. She looked forward to it.

Kenneth drove to Stella Fitzgerald's in Rita's primary car, a silver Chrysler LHS, while she and Daisy sat in the backseat. The women were having a ball. He said, "I can't believe how different my life is whenever I'm in town."

Daisy and Rita spoke the same words at the same time. "What do you mean?"

"In Wichita, I sometimes carry a gun for protection on the job. In Guthrie, I get to drive Miss Daisy and her mama."

Enjoying the moment, Rita said, "And you do it so well."

Kenneth returned her smile. Both women were definite characters. He figured Daisy would

mature in a nearly identical way to her mother
at this age: gracefully, beautifully. He said,
"Don't you two feel weird riding in the backseat
when everybody knows who you are and that a
strange man is driving?"

Daisy said, "Anybody who knows this car be-
longs to Mom also knows exactly who you are.
It's a small town, remember. Besides, neither
one of us wants to be in the car with Mom behind the wheel."

Rita was indignant. "Hey!"

"Mom," Daisy said, "when you drive and talk
at the same time, I get nervous."

Kenneth laughed. "She can't be that bad,
Daisy."

Daisy gave him an oh-you-best-believe-it look.
"When Mom talks and drives, we end up going
someplace we never intended. If we're driving
to Jim's Super Thrift for groceries, chances are
high Mom will be talking and miss the turnoff."

Kenneth tried to control his grin but failed.
"So, when your mom's talking and driving,
you're talking and not paying attention to
where you're going, either. Why else would you
both miss the right turnoff to the grocery store
or any other place?"

Rita gave Kenneth the thumbs-up sign. "He's
right. But to be honest, so are you, Daisy. I know
somebody in at least every two cars I pass on
my way to anywhere in town. I'm always waving
at people and talking at stoplights or something, but I've never had an accident or even
a traffic ticket so I must not be all that bad."

"Touché, Mom, and I didn't mean to get you upset. I'm just a little nervous about this meeting with Stella. Truth is, you and Kenneth are keeping me grounded this week. I'm glad he's here to drive us around."

Delighted, Kenneth tipped an imaginary hat. There was always a reason to smile in Daisy's company. "My pleasure."

Rita said, "You're lucky I'm not twenty years younger."

Daisy said, "If you were twenty years younger I wouldn't be here."

Rita smiled benignly. "I know."

Kenneth laughed, something he'd been doing ever since the three of them had climbed into Rita's car together. "You two are more like sisters than mother and daughter." He meant this as a compliment.

Daisy said, "Not quite. Growing up, Mom always made sure I understood where the line between mother and daughter rested. She's always made herself available to me, but not at the expense of her own goals."

Rita chimed in. "I've always believed that Daisy was her own person, and so from the beginning, I treated her as if our relationship was temporary."

Kenneth frowned. "Temporary?"

Rita recognized the concern in his voice. "Maybe that's the wrong word but basically I mean that I've always known that my guardianship was a short time in a long life span. I knew I had dibs on at least the first eighteen years of

Daisy's life and that whatever happened next was on her efforts and not mine.

"Once she finished high school, there was no guarantee or pressure for her to attend college. While it's true that my role as a parent is for life, my role as her guardian was officially over when she finished high school. By temporary, I mean that there's a line between love and duty. It was my duty to be her guardian and protector, but as a parent, it is my honor to love her. I couldn't have asked for a better daughter than Daisy."

Wearing an oh-I-get-it look, Kenneth said, "Now I understand the calmness in Daisy. One of the things I like best about her is that she's so well centered and balanced. Self-contained. When I'm with her, I don't feel pressure to be her everything. She's strong on her own and she's got a life of her own and when we're together it feels good because we each have something special to bring to the table."

"Special, my foot," Rita said. "You both enjoy your freedom."

Kenneth laughed, but he didn't agree with Rita's statement. Unlike him, Daisy couldn't finish a job and take time off. Her job was daily. He'd been around long enough to notice that plants needed frequent watering and deadheading and shifting for appropriate lighting.

Plants that were sold had to be replaced so that her stock looked full and fresh at all times, something Daisy believed spoke of quality service and merchandise. Her level of freedom was more a way of feeling than a manner of living.

He said, "In her own way, Daisy is as daring as I am as a private detective. She never backs down from a challenge and she's a fighter."

Rita said, "Speaking of detective work. I think something fishy is going on with Stella. She's acting more strange than usual."

Kenneth said, "In what way?"

"She's such an airhead to start off—"

Daisy rolled her eyes. "Mom!"

"—which is why I almost didn't catch on that she's up to something."

There were ominous implications in Rita's statement. The private investigator in Kenneth stood up and took notice. He said, "Like what?"

Rita was flattered by the shift in his attitude: still friendly but now, his demeanor had a keenly inquisitive air. "Beats me. That's why I wanted to ride with you guys over here. We ran into each other at the Sandstone Cottage— that's a hair salon—this morning and she says she found out something interesting on Kandi Kane, but we were both rushing and so I didn't get to find out what she knows."

Daisy was worried. "I hope it isn't serious. This event has the power to kick my business into high gear."

"Yeah," Rita said, "a gear so high you might need to hire somebody full-time to help you out."

"Mom," Daisy said, "I love you dearly, but

you talk too much whenever you pitch in at the garden shop.''

''I wasn't suggesting that I work in your shop,'' Rita said, emphasis on the word *I.* She also wiggled her eyebrows suggestively.

Kenneth struggled to keep the laughter out of his voice. ''I think your mom is referring to me working for you, not herself.''

One thing Daisy couldn't stand was open manipulation. Her mother was crossing some serious lines, first with the house-hunting business and now this. ''Mostly I don't need anybody except a part-timer during busy seasons or special events.''

''That's where I come in,'' Kenneth said. He was aware that Daisy was a little perturbed, but the conversation was too good, too informative to stop. ''You don't know squat about carpentry, which I'm proud to say I do because it means I'll definitely be a contributor and not just somebody 'helping' you out. Since meeting you, I've come to enjoy spending time in your garden.''

''My business,'' Daisy said.

''He's right,'' Rita said. ''Your garden. The business and the house are like the yard ornaments you tuck between the bushes, like the stone hippo and the bird feeders on fence posts that you use for decoration. It's almost as if the house and the business are incidental to the gardens.''

Daisy smiled. ''That's exactly the look I aim

for but you're the first person to say anything about it or even notice.''

"I didn't at first, but with all the commotion going on lately about the garden show, I started to really look at the business," Rita said. "You know how it is when you see something so much that you forget sometimes how special it is. That's what happened to me. Now I see it as other people would and I'm so proud to say you're my daughter. It makes every struggle I had to raise you worthwhile.''

Kenneth winked. "Was she that much of a hellion?''

"No. But any time a woman takes the time to raise a child, she gives up part of herself in the process. I hate to hear arguments about the pros and cons of women working inside or out-side the home and which is better for children.

"It takes money to raise a family. Women have always worked, whether they made money at it or their husbands did. It's kind of like the house and property in Daisy's garden, necessary but incidental to the garden itself. Daisy is my garden. All the dreams I had were passed on to her and she's surpassed anything I wanted for myself or for her.''

"And what did you want for the both of you?'' Kenneth asked.

"Independence. Self-reliance. Financial ease. Land ownership.''

Kenneth said, "She's definitely acquired all those things and more. The same can be said for you.''

"Thank you," Rita said. "I guess the main thing I wanted for Daisy is to realize that whatever man she chose for herself, it should be someone who complemented her and added to whatever she provided for herself. I believe she's chosen well."

Kenneth smiled. "Thank you."

"My only problem with you is that you live too far away."

"Not for long."

"Good."

Kenneth was starting to feel warm and mushy and he didn't like it. "Let's get back to Stella and whatever you think she's hiding."

"Yeah," said Daisy. "You guys are talking about me like I'm not here."

Rita said, "There's nothing wrong with your voice. You could've spoken up at any time."

"I know. I guess I like seeing you two get along. You're the most important people in my life right now."

Rita threw up her hands. "Enough of this mutual admiration society stuff. Let's get the skinny on Stella."

Kenneth escorted both women to Stella's front door. Unbeknownst to the women, he'd been thankful of their conversation. It showed they accepted him into the family, that they trusted him with their secrets, and that they valued his contributions to their small inner circle, as a man and as a friend.

One thing he'd learned in the past was that meeting and falling in love with a woman was one thing; meeting and falling in love with her family was something entirely different. Right now it meant the world to Kenneth.

His easygoing relationship with Daisy's mother was another good sign that he was on the right track about moving to Guthrie. Moving to such a small town was a big decision that couldn't be made entirely on the love of a good woman.

He'd be a fool to think Daisy was everything he wanted in life, even though she was everything he wanted in a woman. Having a partner who worked independently in a profession that made her happy meant that in the spare time they had between them, they could spend it on the pursuit of their private, mutual pleasures.

On this particular trip to Guthrie, Kenneth was content to contain his private pleasures with Daisy to the seclusion of her bedroom in the hours between dusk and dawn, her version of quiet time.

Her lifestyle was relaxed as a general rule but she was seldom alone. Her business was catering to the public and for her, quiet time meant alone time. For Kenneth, those late-night hours with Daisy were about rejuvenation. At the moment, she was all business. That she could compartmentalize so effectively intrigued him.

Stella Fitzgerald greeted Daisy with a smile, one which included Kenneth. For Rita, she simply sniffed once and tossed her head. "Daisy," she said, "I wasn't expecting your . . . friends to show."

"Is there a problem?"

"No. I'm just surprised to see her here."
Stella threw a thumb in Rita's direction but she
didn't look at her. "Shocked is more like it."
Her face turned sly. "However, a real journalist
is always open to surprise encounters. They
might lead to unique revelations."

Rita rolled her eyes. "Speak plain English,
will you?"

Stella spoke in a singsong voice. "I know
something you don't know."

Rita shook briefly with fake laughter. It
stopped as abruptly as it started. "Spoken by a
frustrated singer and ex-housewife who plays at
being a journalist." She added at a lower octave,
"We don't move in the same circles so what you
know is probably irrelevant to me."

Stella shoved her sleeves up and shifted from
foot to foot. She was clearly incensed. "You always piss me off, Rita. You no-class wanna-be."

Rita mentally counted to seven before she
said anything. She hadn't wanted to strike another person so bad in years. "Wanna-be what?"

"Me."

Daisy said, "I always knew you weren't fond
of each other, but—"

Rita shivered delicately with distaste. "Stella
and I have an . . . understanding."

"Yeah," Stella said, her anger scarcely under
wraps. "We understand apples don't fall too far
from the tree."

When Rita bucked up as if she was preparing
herself to punch Stella in the face, Kenneth

stepped between the women and said, "Whoa. What's going on here?"

Rita huffed as if she'd been running. "She started it."

"I did not."

"When we ran into each other at the beauty salon earlier, you hinted that you knew something I should know and now that I'm here to find out what it is, you're acting like the class-act bitch you always were and always will be."

Stella launched into a song so loud, Daisy almost covered her ears. Instead she said to Stella, "I'll call you." To her mom and Kenneth, she said, "Let's go."

Rita didn't budge. She sang right back, but the song was all made up and made sense to Stella and nobody else. It was the weirdest fight scene Kenneth had ever witnessed and he wasn't sure if he should laugh or referee.

Judging by the way Daisy narrowed her eyes and kept glancing from one woman to another, he surmised she was thinking the same thing. She even took two steps closer to her mother who glared at Stella Fitzgerald the way an opera singer might glare at a rival.

But then, something occurred to him as the women sang insults and curses to each other about lost loves and lost dreams, a duel of words that led Kenneth to believe that Rita had stolen Stella's man at some point, a man with eyes as lively as the daughter she never had.

Rita responded to the end of the song by singing that if the man had truly belonged to another woman he could never have belonged to her in the first place. Finders keep and losers weep, she sang, and to Kenneth's astonishment, Stella stopped singing as abruptly as she had started, grabbed Daisy by the arm, and said, "All may not be as it seems. Don't trust your eyes."

Embarrassed and at odds about what to do with her own mother, Daisy hummed the theme song from the television classic, *The Twilight Zone.* "We've all fallen into some parallel reality where familiar things stop making sense."

Kenneth had misgivings. His short trip to visit Daisy had the unsettling undertone of a crime on the verge of happening. These women were feuding over something. He had the ugly suspicion that what they fought over was Daisy.

Six

Back at Daisy's house in her living room, Kenneth put everything that happened behind them, at least for a little while. He did this because Daisy was completely out of sorts. She was fidgety and frowning, and if she said anything at all, her tone was short.

In this transition period, he watched her with a stillness that allowed him to focus on her every physical detail. She was exquisite, more fascinating to him than any other woman he had ever been intimate with in terms of sex and friendship.

His arousal reminded him of how easily they fit together, and even though he longed to join with her now, he allowed himself the intense luxury of scrutiny, the measure of his own desire and of hers.

For Kenneth, mental stimulation was a vital requisite to physical foreplay, which in turn was his favorite prelude to lazy, lingering, and luscious rounds of lovemaking with the only woman who'd been able to capture his heart and hang on to it.

A hint of discontent flickered across his

mind. He was not a man prone to following hunches, but the odd feeling prevailed that she or someone she knew could be in danger, and he felt powerless to stop it. What made him feel strong was the solid comfort that she trusted him; even when she was angry, she trusted him.

In honor of this profound brand of faith, almost spiritual in nature, Kenneth sought to protect her in any and every way that he could. To do this, he had to find a way to be centered, a way to hold his own and master his environment.

This is how it came to be that he was learning more about flowers and exhibitions than he'd ever wanted to know. Flowers were beautiful, but he'd been living without them and could continue living without them if it weren't for the fact that having them around made Daisy so happy. Because flower growing and selling were the framework and setting of Daisy's life, Kenneth was slowly making them part of his own.

Making her happy and seeing her smile because of his interest was worth the time and effort it took to learn something new. He'd never worked this hard, with such single-minded purpose for the sole benefit of one woman's happiness. In some ways, it was a humbling experience, to open himself up so freely to another person's habits and dreams.

Her manner contemplative, Daisy watched him watching her, the possessive, almost feral quality in his eyes so distinctive and volatile that she felt physically branded. This was no casual man with careless caresses in store for her.

Every stroke of his eyes across the exposed parts of her flesh made her feel more lovely than any word could possibly express. But it was his touch that she needed, his touch she intended to savor for as long as her body was able to match him kiss for kiss, stroke for stroke. No other man filled her so completely, her heart and soul as satisfied as her body when he rested, hot and hard between her soft, sweetly scented thighs.

Inside the cool, restful quiet of her bedroom, Kenneth shed his clothing with sensual deliberation. He was aware of the rough fabric of his olive-green shorts, the soft cotton of his shirt, the classic white briefs. The air around him was whipped gently by the fan above Daisy's brass bed. The hairs on his body seemed to tingle along with the taut muscles beneath his dark skin. He was ready.

Daisy's heart pounded. Her pulse raced. The pressure in her blood soared, the sound of it roaring in her ears as she undressed before the lively, territorial eyes of her lover. More swift than he'd been, she stripped away her summer top and Levi's jeans. Off came the lavender-colored bra and matching lace panties. She felt wonderfully alive, the ends of her very soul already in touch and in tune with the man she treasured.

This incredibly sumptuous feeling only magnified itself when deftly, boldly, Kenneth pulled her into the tempered strength of his bare arms. He felt good: hard where she was soft, thick where she was slender, heavy where she was light.

His tongue, hot and probing, penetrated the wet sheath of her lips, traced over the slick enamel of her teeth, alternately dueled and danced with the whip that was her flexing tongue. Every taste was delicious, every sigh was simply marvelous. They needed no words, no music as they swayed together, their bodies moving to a rhythm so old that it exceeded the very concept of time.

In two beats he'd joined them together. The sensations of hot, soft, slick, wet, warm and feminine were an explosive mix of raw sensuality. All the wrongs of the day were made right again, all the odd premonitions of danger were temporarily laid to rest.

He almost exploded then, almost, but for Kenneth, it was much too soon to end the moment, much too soon. And yet, for her, the explosions had only just begun. He raised her in his arms again, high, his strength superior, then brought her down, hard, and it was she who came apart, she who clung to him tightly as passion spun her mind into sexual orbit, as she screamed his name again . . . and again.

It wasn't over, no, not yet, as gently, reverently, he lay her down until her back rested against the covers. But she was far too restless and wound up to languish there against the plush bedding as he did all the slippery sweet work.

She pulled him close to her breast and held him tight, their hearts beating fast, yet in rhythm together, and during those moments of easy quiet interlude, Daisy fell apart again. He captured her groan, the sound low and deep, with a kiss so wonderful that they shared the same sensations: soul-satisfying completeness, a spiritual declaration of love, a binding baptism of faith, each for the other, that both mystified and fascinated as they lingered over their ability to be one.

There was a single moment left and the moment belonged exclusively to him. Daisy rolled him over, his back against the covers. And now it was her strength that was superior to his as she raised her hot, moist self above him, then slowly, ever so slowly joined them together once again.

She brought him to the brink of meltdown, then stopped, using her arms and legs and lips and tongue to erase all thought—past, present, and future—from his mind so that only she was his universe, only she was his beginning and end.

When he could stand the sweetness no longer, she increased the pace, her fingers digging into his shoulders, his fingers gripping the warm roundness of her pretty brown behind as harder, deeper, faster they went until they shimmied and shook and shattered . . . together.

Two hours later, sated and rested, they reentered the everyday world. They were sitting in the living room, and the house was quiet, but outside, the cicadas were keeping up their usual evening-hour racket.

However, it wasn't the sound of the cicadas that captured and sharpened Kenneth's interest, it was the sound of the mockingbirds, their songs original and always tireless. He admired their skill and dedication to their craft of survival among the fittest.

Kenneth felt the same way about Daisy, that she was original and relentless about maintaining her freedom, about developing her skill as a master gardener. A woman like her could be mimicked, but never duplicated. This made her one of his favorite women to know and to love, the kind of woman he'd remember for the rest of his life.

With Rita at her own home, he and Daisy were able to converse openly between themselves. He spoke softly into the comfortable cool of the living room. "What happened at Stella Fitzgerald's place?"

"Some serious drama that we don't need right now," Daisy said. She sounded a little perturbed by his question and it showed in her stiff mannerisms. She sat up straighter; her hands were tight and her eyes had a hard edge to them.

If she was relentless about holding on to her independence, he was relentless about figuring out what made her tick. He didn't raise his voice. He wasn't commanding, but neither did he leave loose strands alone. He made tidy little mental stacks of them, sorted and weighed them, got on Daisy's nerves with them.

He picked them up with his mind, studied them for meaning, then put them back down again, as he did now with the weird episode that had taken place at Stella Fitzgerald's modest house. Daisy wished they didn't have to get into this potentially explosive scene, but she knew it was necessary.

Solid relationships were built on mutual interests, made strong by surviving challenges that tested their strength. Some couples broke up when the going got tough, some couples kept going until mutual ground was met, new foundations laid, better walls designed, reinforced with further challenges and greater tests. It was what being in a committed relationship was all about: truth, faith, honor, and goodness.

She said, "What do you wanna know?"

Kenneth wasn't sure what he wanted to hear about first. Much had gone on in a short time, especially at Stella's. If he hadn't been there, he wouldn't have thought it possible for grown women to behave in such a crazy, ridiculous manner.

His impromptu visit to see Daisy had been peppered with scenes he'd expect to find in an opera—two song-battling divas fighting over what, he didn't know. On top of that, the woman he loved didn't mind sharing her bed with him as long as he kept his visit short.

The cast of characters he had to deal with in this crash course of Garden Exhibiting 101 had colorful names like Kandi, Sugar, Zenith, Cinnamon, Myrtle, Tilly, Spud, Dillingsworth, and Daisy. When it got down to it, Kenneth figured he might as well add his own name to the mix: Gunn.

"Explain the singing," he finally said. "I even pinched myself during their performance. Couldn't believe what was happening. I still don't."

Daisy kept it simple. "Mom and Stella went to school together. They sang in the school choir. Stella was named in honor of Ella Fitzgerald. Stella sang in the church choir in addition to the school choir. She's known all over Guthrie as a great soloist."

"Let me guess," Kenneth said. "Your mom didn't sing in the choir, so Stella thought she was better than Rita."

"Right."

"But singing like that in public?" He knew it was a scene he'd remember for the rest of his life. Things like that just weren't normal, not even on television, unless it was a musical of some kind.

"It goes back to their senior year in high school," she explained. "They went after the same role in the same musical. Stella ad-libbed during the audition and did some Ella Fitzgerald-styled scat in what should have been a pretty classical performance. Mom just did what was required and she got the part. Stella never forgave her."

Kenneth did a swift mental calculation that

had him rocking his brows up. "That had to have been more than thirty years ago."

He asked the second question that had nagged at him ever since Rita returned Stella's first song. "Have they always dueled with songs?"

"Oh, yeah."

Even after Daisy's explanations, Kenneth couldn't reconcile what he'd witnessed at Stella's with any reality that made sense. The singing women were in their fifties, long past the age he imagined would compete in such a harebrained manner. If they behaved that ridiculous at the garden show, newshound reporters would have a field day.

"If I hadn't seen it for myself," he said, "I wouldn't have believed it. Your mom is so controlled and friendly that I find it hard to believe she's got such a strong enemy, especially someone in a very public profession."

Having spent her life in a city whose population of 10,000 hadn't changed since the Land Run in 1889, Daisy accepted the eccentricities in life at face value. In Guthrie, very little was balanced, its city politics often well-meaning but erratic, its historical society constructive yet flawed by the personal whimsies of a chosen few.

So if her mother and Stella Fitzgerald wanted to sing their anger and blues in front of the Masonic Temple on a summer afternoon, Daisy figured Guthrie was the place to be. And since

Guthrie was home, then so be it. She shrugged as if to say, *What is, is.*

"Mom," she explained, "is the softest quilt in the world over a cast-iron bed with no mattress."

Even though Kenneth laughed, he believed that behind every face was a powerful story. He had a feeling that the story on Daisy's first garden show was destined to be remembered for its colorful supporting characters and its two journalist/horticulturists as it would be remembered for its beautiful show exhibits.

All he'd really wanted to do on this trip was keep the flame burning in his romance with Daisy, wanted to make sure she understood he still cared deeply about her, but from the minute he'd arrived in Guthrie, he'd felt like he was sinking in quicksand, something he'd learned from Spud Gurber actually existed along Oklahoma riverbeds.

If danger did exist in Daisy's little Wonderland, Kenneth would have a terrible time separating the good guys from the bad ones. The problem with Daisy was that she trusted all the oddballs she held in her inner circle.

His unspoken fear was that she might have delegated so many behind-the-scenes aspects of the job at hand that she might be knee-deep in red Oklahoma dirt before her lights came on that trouble lurked in the shadowy corners of her customers' wants and needs. For this reason, Kenneth silently vowed to be as relentless as he felt was necessary to keep her safe.

He said, "I hear you, Daisy, but those two were fighting over something deeper than a high school grudge."

"I keep forgetting you're a detective," she said with disgust. She figured his animal instincts, honed by his work with criminals, must have been in overdrive. It wasn't fair to discount his feelings. "Stella says Mom stole my dad from her. She says I should be her daughter."

"That's crazy."

"Not as crazy as Dad dating Stella after he split up with Mom."

Kenneth took a few moments to take inventory of his conversation with Daisy, a tense talk that functioned somewhere between almost rude and almost polite, but definitely forced. He had never been the kind of man who meddled with other people's lives and emotions without good cause.

In the silence, Kenneth's eyes scanned Daisy's living room, its wonderful combination of purple, red, blue, green and yellow more like jewel tones than crayon colors. In the end, he shook his head in disbelief and said the only thing that came close to reality. "Soap opera city."

"Ain't that the truth."

"What happened to your dad?"

"He tried to get back with Mom after he came to his senses but she told him . . . well, you can imagine what she told him. Dad was history after that. Neither Mom nor Stella would have anything to do with him."

"That must have hurt you a lot when you were a kid."

Almost nonchalantly, Daisy waved her hand in the air as if she were swatting away a fly that was getting too close to her face. Her action pretty much reflected her attitude on the subject in general.

She said, "I had a good life growing up. As long as I had my friends and my parents didn't get into some big tug-of-war over who got dibs on my time, I was okay. I'm not into fighting and arguing, and that's mostly what my parents were doing. Nobody was happy. Now we are. Content anyway."

Ever the analytical thinker, Kenneth put two and two together and came up with four. The bigger handle he got on Daisy, the bigger his attachment to her grew. "Is that why you don't want to get married or live together?"

She made a sour face and shrugged. "Probably. Too risky."

He thought for a minute, his mind picking up and putting down the conversations he'd heard, the events he'd witnessed. At her best, Daisy was inspired and creative. At her worst, she was pessimistic and emotionally blocked, at least when it came to the subject of their commitment.

Despite her don't-give-a-damn attitude, Kenneth was certain that she did. He added acting to her list of social talents. On the one hand, she was a separate and distinct part of the flower show, and on the other hand she was part of the show's song-and-dance routine. She was playing a role and the role had everything to do with looking in control, even if she wasn't, even if some of her friends were off the hook.

"I haven't heard you sing," he said. "Can you?"

She wished he hadn't asked. She preferred to keep the subject and the incident closed. She only entertained his questions this time because the entire situation was new to him. This was a getting-to-know-you grace period as far as she was concerned.

He may have thought she gave a damn, but the truth was, she really didn't, at least not in a profound emotional way. Her mother's life was her mother's life. The fact they were friends and had love for each other was enough for Daisy.

She said, "No. Dad can't sing, either. As it is, I feel like I'm part of a circus act and not a fancy one, either. But, back to the show, which is why Mom and Stella were together in the first place. Stella will do some prelim work with Kandi Kane.

"She'll tie in whatever she gleans that's worthwhile with whatever she picks up at the garden show. It's almost all business. I say almost, because nobody can erase the past and Mom and Stella have a big fat past that puts their egos on the line whenever they come face-to-face. They really are ridiculous but I don't know what to do about them."

He was impressed that she wasn't afraid to let

Stella participate in the garden show. He would have been afraid because he didn't think Stella could be trusted not to act out. "How will you handle her rivalry with your mom?"

Daisy spoke with the confidence of experience. After all, she did have years and years of it and Kenneth was just getting started. She wondered what he'd do if he found out Stella and her mother did things a lot more strange than singing opera-style in public.

They used pureed banana skins to polish their silver, put hair in their compost piles for nitrogen, and they waterproofed their tomato stakes by soaking them in motor oil for twenty-four hours. Just like they competed in song, Rita and Stella competed in home remedies made with common household items.

These women, including Miss Myrtle and Miss Tilly, were the guiding leaders in Daisy's life. All of them were a little odd, all of them lovable, much like the eccentric witch-aunts in the book and film *Practical Magic*.

Over time, Daisy had learned to take odd behavior in stride. After all, she wore green garden clogs the way some women wore flip-flops or bedroom slippers. "They'll be too busy to have a singing match," she advised him. "Kandi Kane can be hell on two feet. Ditto for her daughter, Sugar."

Kenneth was shaking his head and frowning even as he asked the next question. "What is it with those two?"

Daisy knew exactly what he was talking about.

Part of the interest in the garden show for the exhibitors and general public was the possibility of fireworks between the people putting on the show: Stella and Rita, Kandi and Sugar, Daisy and the garden club.

Then there were the people who were mad about not having this flower or that flower featured in the show, people such as Whitney Webb, who wanted veggies on display right alongside the flowers.

Whitney Webb didn't see why the competition couldn't include tomatoes, especially when categories could range from beefsteak size to Roma. She just didn't. But if she had to settle on showing off her rubra rosa rugosas, then she would, hairy thorns and all.

Daisy knew she couldn't please everybody and had never set out to try. She did work at being nice, no small task this close to the action, but when she convinced people such as Whitney Webb to participate in spite of their misgivings, she felt fantastic.

With this thought in mind, Daisy jerked an I'm-determined-to-get-along-with-you-even-if-it-kills-me look on her face and smiled at Kenneth as if life couldn't get any better than it was right at that precise moment. She sought clarification to his question. "You mean, what is it with those two, as in Kandi and Sugar, outside of their corny names?"

"Yeah."

Daisy believed that the more background Kenneth had, the better he'd be able to assist her during crunch time. This was crunch time. "Kandi is beautiful and abrasive, a celebrity garden buff who also happens to be a nasty gossip, the kind of gossip people love to hate even while they love to hear what she has to say."

Kenneth took a couple of seconds to digest this information. Had he been in Wichita, he doubted he'd be having this much excitement. Most of his cases were very ordinary, very routine. He seldom chased after robbers or murderers although he did look for bail jumpers on occasion.

He often functioned as a go-between, such as serving subpoenas in tricky situations. Once he'd been able to make the money exchange for a kidnap victim that happened to be a nanny and the child she'd been hired to keep safe while their politician parents managed dual careers. Kenneth liked his job, enjoyed the versatility of it.

There was nothing routine about Daisy Rogers, and she was the most important case of his life, a case of the heart. Behind that smooth façade of the laid-back gardener was a quick-thinking mind and a sharp decision maker.

He said after some serious thought, "This Kandi Kane character sounds like Howard Stern or Rush Limbaugh."

Daisy gave a little snort that was part comedy and part oh-please. "There's also Martha Stewart or Joan Rivers. Both women create strong public opinion, just like Kandi Kane. Regardless of whether or not people love or hate her, they do find themselves listening to what Kandi has to say."

"So Sugar Kane rides on her mother's coat-tails the way Melissa Rivers hangs on to her mother's," Kenneth decided. He said it more as a statement than a question.

"You've got it," Daisy said. She liked the way he cut through the muck of a problem in such short order. "Sugar spends a lot of her time doing damage control behind her mother. Then again, like Stella says, the apple doesn't fall far from the tree."

"Meaning?"

Daisy chose her words carefully. Her opinion carried a lot of weight with Kenneth because he trusted her basic common sense. He also expected her to be fair. She couldn't be partial; she had to look at issues with candid reasoning, even if she wasn't in the mood for introspection, such as right now.

She said, "Sugar really tries to be good, but she has this nasty habit of making off-color remarks that don't win her any praise. Some people call brutal honesty being up-front, when many times, total honesty is rude. Sugar is princess-pretty, but that mouth of hers ain't nothing nice."

Kenneth leaned back against the sofa, arms crossed over his chest, eyes glittering with steel-hard intelligence. His mind was locked into the puzzle of the inner workings of Daisy's inner circle like a pigeon on its way home.

He said, "I see what you mean about your mom having her hands full during the garden show. Stella sings. Kandi gripes. Sugar insults people. Rita will control them, as much as they can be controlled anyway, while you concentrate on the smooth running of the garden show, your garden club members acting as soldiers among the troops. In this case, the troops are exhibitors, the general public, and your regular customers."

Daisy's smile had two extra watts. "Right."

"Is this project worth your while financially?" He'd been wondering about this ever since he saw the layout she'd planned for the event, from the physical props to the flyers on the tables and the forms used for judging.

She paused before saying, "In the long run, yes. But I'd be lying if I didn't admit I've had second thoughts about the whole thing on more than one occasion. It's kind of like planning a little wedding that turns into a big wedding that makes the bride and groom want to elope. I'm doing my best to keep things simple."

Kenneth reasoned that simple issues were one of something, they were not complex or compound in nature. While he believed that Daisy had lived a life of grace, he didn't think there was too much that was truly simple about it. A smile lit up his eyes. "I've never known you to have doubts about anything."

Her eyes smiled right back. "When Shanita Lynne, one of my regular customers, demanded to know why vegetables were excluded from the exhibition, I almost caved in and let her have

them. She called me at home. She talked to me
at the post office. She talked to me at Near and
Far—"

Kenneth held up a hand in the halt position.
It was the only indication he wasn't as relaxed
as he appeared. People who weren't salesmen
and who didn't take no for an answer made
him wary. In his experience, pushy people were
obsessive about their desires and pet peeves.
"Wait a minute. What is Near and Far? I think
you told me once, but—"

"It's only one of my favorite stores in Guthrie," Daisy said, realizing that she and Kenneth
still had a lot of sightseeing to do. "I like the
store because it has unusual gifts and great candles and pretty stationery. It's downtown over
on the west side of Harrison, right next door
to Granny Had One. You remember Granny's,
don't you?"

"Yeah," he said, arms folded across his chest
again, legs straight out and crossed at the an-
kles. This was about as relaxed as he was going
to get when it came to this garden show business. He thought Daisy had bitten off more
than she could chew and was just too stubborn
to admit it. "It's a restaurant."

Daisy knew full well he wasn't thrilled with
this new twist in the behind-the-scenes shenanigans she'd been privately dealing with before
he arrived to visit. She wondered idly if he
wished he'd postponed his trip to see her by
two weeks. She didn't want to hear the answer,
so she didn't plan on asking the question. His

crossed arms and legs said a lot: Kenneth Gunn was not a happy camper. She cleared her throat and said, "Right."

Kenneth was continually amazed at how worked up the locals were about Daisy's endeavor. "And this Shanita Lynne approached you about vegetables even when you told her no, not once but several times?" He said this with a note of incredulity in his tone.

Daisy said, "That about covers it."

In Kenneth's experiences, people who presumed to know more than they should were often the most obnoxious to be around. He didn't have a good feeling about this Shanita Lynne character: where there was one, there were others just like her. "It's a flower show, not a dinner for the President."

While it was true that Daisy was fanatical about her work, she tried not to be so self-absorbed that she failed to consider other points of view. Shanita Lynne was persistent but she also had a strong, very realistic perspective when it came to getting what she wanted. She was also a good friend and steady customer, pushy but not harmful.

If she needed to hear the word no ten times in order to believe it, then she'd hear it ten times. Some people subscribed to the notion that the squeaky wheel got the grease, and Shanita Lynne was one of those people.

"I know," Daisy said, "but like I always say, many people in Guthrie think growing flowers just because they're beautiful is a waste of time. Vegetable gardening is what's traditional here."

Astute, Kenneth discerned the heart of Daisy's problem. "If you'd had a vegetable show or festival then your garden club members would get ticked off."

Even though she had been reluctant to begin the conversation, Daisy was grateful to have a sounding board. Kenneth really knew how to listen, how to make just the right comments at just the right time. Some days, like this, Daisy felt alienated from the garden club.

As its leader, she couldn't afford to speak this freely for fear she might upset someone by saying the wrong thing at the wrong time. "Precisely." She paused slightly before adding, "Then there's Billy the Window Washer."

"Okay, Alice," Kenneth said as he shook his head, "who else is in Wonderland?" His intellectual curiosity was thoroughly activated. He was a long way from being bored with the backstage machinations of the garden show.

All this talking was productive for Daisy. Like a good massage, it freed her mind of stress, subtle strain she hadn't been consciously aware of before Kenneth opened her up for brainstorming-style conversation. She hoped they would always be able to speak this freely, looked forward to it. "Billy wants to park cars and wash windows while guests are at the flower show."

"Enterprising young man."

"Yes," Daisy said, her mind conjuring up an image of Billy Maxwell. He was short, well-built, and kept his head bald. One of his front teeth had a gold star and he was determined to make it big as a foreign-news correspondent. She couldn't imagine him doing anybody's dirty work.

She said, "He just graduated as a senior from high school and occasionally helps with odd jobs around the shop. When I told him I didn't need help with the props and whatever because you're here, he opted to direct cars for me and wash windows in the process."

"Where'd he get the name Billy the Window Washer?" Kenneth was almost afraid to ask the question.

"His buddies," Daisy said. She was fully aware that Kenneth was picking and choosing his questions with the utmost care. She would, too, if she were in his shoes. He thought his best girl was as nutty as her friends. "Don't forget, he just got out of high school. He's been washing cars as a side business for years."

Kenneth believed that the best way to get from understanding to fulfillment was knowledge. Knowledge was gained through perception. Perception was achieved by assessing odd mental images. His troubled mind ran over the most pressing oddities that stood out.

Stella Fitzgerald, the songbird and local journalist who got her facts mixed up with her fiction.

The garden club, twenty members strong, and highly possessive of Daisy and the garden show itself.

Rita Rogers, a woman he considered the queen of discretion until she entered the insane battle of song with her archrival, Stella.

Sugar Kane, a woman who tried to do the right thing but often failed. Why else would she sing her blues instead of stating her feelings plainly?

Kandi Kane, celebrity garden buff who rubbed everyone the wrong way.

Daisy, tired, excited—was she too relaxed, too trusting of the people she called her friends?

He said, "High school is a recurring theme here. Rita's rivalry with Stella stems from high school."

"It's a small town," Daisy pointed out. "Big grudges are born and raised in places like this. We all know about the Hatfields and the McCoys."

"I bet Billy sees and hears a lot around town," Kenneth said. "In my line of work, I've noticed that people tend to ignore hired help and the young. Imagine the conversations he must overhear in parking lots while he's washing windows. Add to the fact that he's a kid, he'd be practically invisible."

"Never thought of it that way," Daisy said.

"I want to meet him."

She had the awful idea Kenneth had developed doubts about her ability to judge people safely and with relative accuracy. Her business was built largely on her ability to think straight and strong. She sought to reassure him, but she wasn't sure she'd be able to pull it off. "I know my mom and those guys are a little strange but you can't possibly be expecting any real problems around here."

Kenneth did trust her judgment. She had once believed in him when no one else would have touched him. He just didn't trust anybody else, including her mother, Rita, who had a serious problem with Stella, who had a serious problem with Kandi Kane, who might pose a serious problem for Daisy. For Kenneth, these were red flags.

He said, "It doesn't hurt to have somebody looking out for trouble spots. I want this window washer guy to report anything unusual he sees or hears."

Daisy made a face at his commanding attitude. As far as she was concerned, this was still her turf, her show, her life. Granted, Kenneth was her lover, but he was also a visitor. He got to stay at her house because she wanted him there. Whether this was his last visit or not was up to her. She had to be on good behavior, but his had to be better. She said with spunk, "He should report to me and not to you."

Kenneth knew she was having a hard time sharing her carefully constructed power, but he wasn't about to pretend trouble wasn't in the air. His sixth sense was screaming and he was the kind of man who followed his instincts.

In his line of work, instincts were backed up and sorted out with on-target questioning, such as the probing he was doing with Daisy, what he considered a mild, informal interview. What he wanted from her were facts, details, observations about what she felt or heard or wanted to do during the final moments of the garden show exhibition.

He was finding out that Daisy was good at keeping secrets, that she was loyal to a fault, that she didn't like her authority or her opinion questioned. Neither did he, and he figured that bottom line was the juice that fueled their current argument.

He said, "This fellow should report to me because I'll have the time and presence of mind to troubleshoot problems. You'll be occupied with the details of the show."

She hated to admit it, but he was right. A respectable leader knew when to seek help and when to delegate. It was time to delegate and Kenneth was the perfect guy to trust with the level of responsibility and constructive thinking she needed in order to succeed. "They're also competitive."

"That's what I mean," Kenneth said, "I checked the podium. The surface was pretty rough. I sanded it down but before I could varnish it, the wood had been roughed up again. It couldn't have been an accident."

She shrugged her left shoulder in a negligent manner. "Maybe you only thought you'd buffed out the podium."

"That wouldn't be possible. I'm not a forgetful person and that's a time-intensive project that's not something I'd forget or even half do. Kandi Kane will use that podium, right?"

Daisy didn't like where this conversation was headed. "Right," she said, her tone leaning toward the cautious side.

In contrast, Kenneth's mind was racing. Deliberate destruction or interference with the running of the show was a serious red flag to him that the enemy-plagued Kandi Kane might be in some sort of danger, even if the danger was only in the form of a practical joke or some other stunt designed to throw her off guard and make her look bad in front of an assembled audience of her peers.

If that was the case, Stella Fitzgerald would be in a good position for an up-close-and-personal story, just the kind she wanted for her new style of writing for the society pages. It wasn't way off base to think she might engineer a headline-making story about Kandi Kane to launch her society column. If that was so, then Daisy required tighter security than she first imagined.

"Who else has had access to the podium area?"

"Mostly the garden club ladies."

Kenneth rubbed his chin in thought. "I also noticed two wobbling chairs at the keynote table."

"Only two?" she asked. Kenneth was getting so edgy he was making her edgy right along with him. It was like watching lightning in the sky and hearing thunder, only to have the storm pass right on by.

"This is serious," he warned. He noticed that her eyes were smoky, defiant in their boldness.

She said, "I'm sure there's more." She didn't say it nice and she didn't mean it nice. Her face was too calm, her manner too controlled. She didn't want to hear about problems at this late stage. Her resources were at the limit, even with Kenneth's help.

"The wobbling chairs were at either end of the table. Usually the keynote speaker sits at the head of the table, right?"

"In this case, yes."

"What if someone is sabotaging the garden show? Not knowing which end of the table Kandi would sit at wouldn't be a problem if both ends are screwed over. Same thing with the podium. But since Kandi would be at the podium the longest, it's easy to think she'd be the first to really make use of it."

"What in the flip are you talking about, Kenneth?"

"Come on, Daisy. I'm saying that Kandi Kane would be the most likely person to get comfortable enough to lean on the surface or whatever than someone doing a casual, brief introduction. That person would be you."

Daisy hummed the *Twilight Zone* theme song. It was either hum or put her hands over her ears in order to put Kenneth on mute.

In turn, he didn't care if she got up and danced, just so long as she stayed in the living room and heard him out. He had no intention of backing down from his line of questioning. "Who set the chairs at that particular table?"

"Me and Stella and a couple of garden club ladies."

The back of Kenneth's mind produced a viable scenario. "One of them could be making trouble for you. I've got a likely candidate in mind."

"Don't tell me, it's Stella."

"That's exactly the person I'm thinking about," he said. "Stella would have a lot to gain if Kandi took a wrong turn."

Daisy rolled her eyes. She couldn't believe how suspicious Kenneth was getting. This was Guthrie. She had no enemies in Guthrie. She was on cordial speaking terms with everybody she could think of, including Kandi Kane.

"Uh-huh," she said. "With you trailing Stella around, you won't be paying attention to the real saboteur, if there is one, and I don't think there is."

"It's what I'm thinking, too. I can't spend the day following one person."

His casual statement shocked her. "I was joking."

"I wasn't."

Daisy sighed in disgust. She felt as if they were on a Ferris wheel going round and round, faster and faster, getting no place fast. She could think of something better to do, like going to Brahm's for a medium-size peach malt, or going to Sonic for a Route 44 green apple slush.

She eyed him the same way she'd considered a grade school pest she wanted to shove to the side or against the blackboard. "You are out of control."

"No, I'm not. I want this window washer guy to be on the lookout for trouble spots," Kenneth said. "He's familiar to you. He's obviously well liked or he wouldn't be in business on your property. Basically, I want him where I can see him. He's someone that will have free access to the event without anyone in particular overseeing what he does. That can be an asset to you."

Feeling her control shift dramatically, Daisy put her foot down. What he did in her house was one thing, what he did in public, in relation to her, was something else. "I won't have my guests or my help spied on, Kenneth."

He flexed his muscles, both mental and physical. He didn't want her to feel dominated but more than that, he didn't want to see her hurt, which he was beginning to think could easily happen if her guard was down among people she valued as friends. From experience, he knew this could be deadly.

While working as a police officer in Wichita, Kenneth had discovered that one of his closest friends was selling stolen weapons on the side to make extra money to pay for his card game gambling habits. Since then, Kenneth realized that even good men could make bad choices given the right mix of greed and desperation. His faith in his friend had affected his level of trust, something he relied on heavily while out on patrol.

He also realized that sometimes friends harbored jealousy that could prove harmful or fatal if the wrong nerve was struck. Animosity made friends deadly adversaries because they had access to personal secrets. What secrets did Daisy have that might have an adverse affect on her life in the very near future?

He said, "I won't have you in jeopardy, either. Something strange is going on around Guthrie and the closer you get to opening your show, the weirder things become. I don't like the idea someone is screwing around with the staging props."

Daisy was outraged enough to raise her voice. It was one degree short of a flat-out shout. "A podium and two chairs are not props."

"Of course they are," he said. "The stage is the setting you designed to showcase what you want to highlight. Plants and your keynote speaker are the main draws to your function. If someone wanted to hurt you—or your keynote speaker—what better way to do it than to screw around with the high-profile areas of the garden show?"

She folded her arms across her chest and proceeded to close her mind. She said between pinched lips, "I don't have any enemies."

"We all have enemies," Kenneth said. "You're just comfortable with yours, but from everything I've heard about Kandi Kane, she's got enemies all over the place. If she's injured or made to look bad in some way, that reflects, however inadvertently, back on the hostess, in this case, you."

The two glared at each other.

Daisy said, "I don't want to fight with you, Kenneth, but this is crazy. You're supposed to stay in the background. I don't want you messing things up for me. I've worked too hard on this project to see it sabotaged by paranoia."

Kenneth's eyes glittered between narrowed slits. They had taken a dangerous turn together in their relationship. It was as if the great sex they'd shared had never happened. "You don't trust me."

Her eyes slapped him to the ground, hard. "Not when you're talking to me as if you're the one in charge and I'm too simple to maintain even the most basic safety measures. I've known people around here since I could first walk and talk. I don't want you giving my friends some kind of third degree because you're suspicious of everything you don't know or don't understand."

He glared at her. He only wanted the best for her and the best was the truth. "You aren't being fair, Daisy."

She gave him a who-do-you-think-you-are-anyway look. It was hard for her to believe that not so very long ago she'd been riding his naked body like a wild woman and having the time of her life while she was doing it. Talk about night and day.

"I'm being honest," she said. "You can't come into my life and take it over. I don't tell you how to run your business and I don't tell you how to live, so don't start something that will finish us off."

He gave her a you-don't-have-a-clue-about-the-real-world look. "I don't want to fight with you, either, but I know what I'm doing."

She couldn't believe the nerve of him. Suddenly she saw that he walked a thin line between strength and pigheadedness. She was glad to know that the flower show would be over soon and his visit along with it.

This was one of those times when she enjoyed knowing she didn't have to take any crap from anybody unless she wanted to. She could love Kenneth Gunn or leave him if she really wanted to.

She said, "Not about flower exhibitions or running a rose nursery."

"About people, Daisy. All I'm saying is that we should prepare for a worst-case scenario so that if something—"

Daisy jumped up from the sofa and flung her hands in the air. It was all she could do not to chuck the sofa cushions at his head. "Nothing is gonna happen! Nothing! Nothing! Nothing!"

Kenneth watched as she stomped out of the living room and out the front door in a huff. As he did, he wondered why everyone spoke as if Kandi Kane was a hard case when she'd been very polite while visiting with Daisy. What was Kandi Kane trying to hide?

Seven

It was Thursday, the day of the gardening show. "You're so lucky," Zenith said to Daisy as they surveyed the exhibition.

Overall, Daisy was pleased that everything and everybody appeared to be in the right place. The conversation level was high and excited. It surprised her that her best girlfriend would be so serious at a happy time like this. All their hard work was paying off in a major way and Daisy couldn't imagine what would bring such a wistful note to Zenith's voice. "Why?"

"Kenneth," she said. "He adores you."

Daisy angled a quick look at her handsome lover. He was talking to one of her favorite customers, Mr. Dillingsworth, an elderly gentlemen who enjoyed one-upping Zenith at her garden shop when it came to buying the freshest plants. Both of them liked first dibs on flower shipments.

"I have to admit," Daisy said, "Kenneth's been terrific. I don't know how he manages to stay so calm, but I really appreciate it. When things go nuts and then get nuttier around here, all I've got to do is take a quick peek at him and I feel all right again."

Zenith gave her friend's shoulder a squeeze. She and Daisy looked so much alike, they were often mistaken for sisters. Both women dressed similar, in jeans and comfortable cotton tops on most days. On this day, they each wore light-colored slacks and blouses. She said, "You look great."

Daisy shook her head in amazement. They each wore straw hats, only Zenith's hat had a cluster of fake hydrangea attached to it. Daisy's hat bore her namesake flower. "We talked about everything but what we'd wear today."

Zenith laughed. "Cosmic twins." More seriously, she added, "Hey, girlfriend, we're gonna come through this just fine. You'll see."

"I thought Kenneth was being paranoid, Zenith. He was right to think there might be trouble."

Zenith gave Daisy a hug that comforted them both. They'd been best girlfriends forever and would be best girlfriends until the day they died if she had any say about it. It was Daisy who had listened to Zenith's dreams when they were children, Daisy who listened now that they were adults.

With Kenneth on the scene, it appeared that their relationship would evolve into something different, yet equally strong. For the first time in their lives, their friendship would have to be shared by a constant third person.

Zenith said softly and a little teary, "You

know, don't you, that I'll always want what's best for you?"

Daisy said, "I can't put a price on the peace of mind you've given me during this garden show project."

"Hey," Zenith said, "I'm as excited about this thing as you are. I only wish I was competing. My miniroses are gorgeous this year."

Daisy laughed. Zenith literally owned hundreds of miniature roses in her city garden. "They're always gorgeous. It's why I'm glad we excluded our garden club from participating in the event. We can't be judges and exhibitors, too."

Zenith snorted in disgust. "No kidding. There would be all kinds of infighting going on. Doing the show this way makes the garden club feel pride in running a successful event. They couldn't be so objective if they were actually participating. I know I wouldn't be. As far as I'm concerned, I grow the best roses in town."

"And you'd be mad if you didn't win."

Zenith grinned. "Yep."

Daisy continued to scan the event for possible trouble spots. All the key players were in place. As far as she could tell, the exhibitors were pleased with the displays and with the smooth-running registration process. Forty people had checked in and the last five were standing in line.

Kenneth appeared beside her just after Zenith went to answer a question at the registration table. She'd been beckoned over by Cinnamon Hartfeld. "If I didn't know you better, Daisy," he said, "I'd think you were totally at ease."

"I'm a wreck," she admitted.

He edged a little closer to her. "I know."

Daisy suppressed the urge to wring her hands. "Kandi Kane is late."

"I heard."

"Who told you? Mom?"

Kenneth smiled. "Yes. When I talked to her, she was on her way to the house to call Kandi's hotel."

"Kandi's daughter is here."

Kenneth eyed the young woman. "I saw her. I gather she and her mom aren't getting along or they stayed in separate hotels."

Daisy shifted her head to the side and scrunched her face. She'd been making faces all morning. "Man," she said, "you're really good at this detective stuff. Sugar is staying with friends here in town. They live in a bungalow on Cleveland Street."

"She's more pleasant than I expected," Kenneth admitted. He spoke casually but his eyes were constantly roaming, constantly assessing what he saw. His actions and coolly efficient attitude reassured Daisy that everything would turn out right—if only Kandi Kane would get there.

Kandi Kane never made it to the podium; she was found dead in her hotel suite. Daisy received the news from Spud Gurber, the tobacco-chewing officer of the local law, who heard about Kandi's death before the news hungry media.

Dressed in his Guthrie Police Department uniform, he took Daisy to the side and said in a low, just-for-your-ears-only tone, "I suppose this means you'll cancel the rest of the garden show."

"No, she won't," Rita said upon entering the room. They were standing near the entrance. "I'll step into Kandi's shoes."

"No, I will," Stella Fitzgerald said. She'd witnessed Rita's distress and Spud Gurber's patrol car and figured there was some type of melodrama in full swing.

Daisy wasn't in the mood for a quarreling singing match between her mother and Stella. She was reeling from the bombshell dropped by Spud. Despite his lackadaisical attitude, Spud Gurber was smarter than he looked.

He said, "If you can figure out a way to keep your show alive, do it. Otherwise you're going to have pandemonium."

"He's right," Rita said. She looked healthy and elegant in a soft and flowing African print dress. "You'll have refunds galore. Exhibitors will be upset because their prized whatever will never get noticed."

Daisy said, "This isn't about money."

Stella said, "It's always about money."

For the first time, Kenneth was inclined to break his silence. There was so much going on, he was afraid he'd miss something important if he wasn't quiet and careful. He'd been the one who led Spud to Daisy so that they could all develop a damage-control strategy, if such a thing was genuinely possible at this point.

"Money is important and it's a huge concern but I agree with Daisy that more is at stake: her reputation—"

Rita was outraged. "Her what?"

"Reputation," Daisy said. "And guess what, Mom? Kenneth is right. If we don't go through with this flower show and make it a success, we might as well scrap ever doing another one. Word of mouth can make or break a function like this."

Nodding her head sagely, Stella said, "If people say great things about the flower show, attendance will be better next year. If it's bad press, numbers will decline."

"I just wish it wasn't murder! So much is at stake," Rita said as she wrung her hands and paced.

Kenneth raised his hand. "I get the picture. The show must go on." Like the movie *Jaws*, there was a shark in the water, and yet the policy-making officials weren't thinking about safety, they were thinking about the bottom line and image control."

"Right," Rita and Stella said together. Amazed to be in agreement, the women broke into laughter, caught themselves abruptly and stopped. This was no laughing moment: Daisy needed them and Kandi Kane was dead.

Daisy shook her head. "Face it, ladies. The only way I'm gonna pull this thing off is if we all pitch in. Once major media coverage finds out Kandi is dead, the garden shop will become national news."

Rita chuckled. "Looks like your wish to expand the business is set to happen in a way you never expected."

"Murder." Daisy could scarcely say the word, let alone think it.

Kenneth placed both his hands on her shoulders. She felt rigid in his grasp. He said, "We don't know that it's murder."

Rita shuddered. "A woman that young," she said.

"And treacherous—" Stella added.

"—will make headlines no matter what you say or do," Kenneth finished. "You might as well use that platform to apply damage control that will benefit the business."

"He's right, Daisy," Rita said. "It's a cruel world sometimes. Play the cards you've been dealt and get on with your life."

Stepping out of Kenneth's embrace, Daisy said, "Stella, you take Kandi's place as keynote speaker. Mom, you assist Stella any way you can. Kenneth, you're the expert when it comes to drama and . . . and maybe murder. I'd like you to work with Spud Gurber and any other authorities if they'll let you. I'm just worried we'll get some flak from Sugar Kane about going ahead with the flower show."

As it turned out, she couldn't have been

more wrong. Twenty-something Sugar Kane couldn't wait for the police show to begin. She was five feet nine inches tall. Her skin was the color of polished walnut, her hair was long and straight and dark red. Her nails were French manicured, the index of her right finger pointed at Daisy's face when she approached the assembled group at the entrance. "Someone bashed my mother upside the head so hard they killed her."

"So," Kenneth said, "it was definitely murder."

Sugar glared at him the same way she would a cockroach: with disdain and intent to kill. "Who the hell are you?"

"Kenneth Gunn."

"Private detective," Daisy added.

Sugar's eyes did a slow scroll from Kenneth to Daisy to Stella and Rita, back to Kenneth and finally Daisy again. "What the hell is going on here?"

"Kenneth is my—"

"—fiancé," Rita finished.

Daisy couldn't believe her mother's nerve in saying what she just did and her persistence at making Kenneth a permanent part of both their lives.

Before she could open her mouth to set Sugar straight about who was who, Stella said, "Daisy hired Kenneth to look into your mother's death."

Daisy gasped in dismay. No wonder Stella got

her facts mixed up when she reported the news.
"Sugar," she said, "that is not true."

Kenneth took control of the conversation. "I don't want anyone else to get hurt."

Sugar was outraged. "My mother wasn't hurt. She was killed. Somebody around here is gonna pay."

"Why don't you let the police do their job?" Kenneth said.

"Why don't you mind your own business?" Sugar told him.

Daisy thought the other woman might hit him. She said, "Careful, Sugar."

Sugar's look was frigid. "I prefer knowing where I stand," she said. "It's not with either of you."

Kenneth said, "You don't act like a grieving daughter."

Sugar gave him a hard stare. "There's no way you can judge the right or wrong of my attitude. You don't know me from jack."

Kenneth didn't like her at all and it showed on his face. "I think you know something about the murder."

Instead of answering, Sugar stalked off.

Kenneth let her go. His intelligence was honed by years spent dealing with desperate criminals, fearful victims, and mistakes made by normally law-abiding citizens. It was chilling to think a murderer might be hiding in plain sight.

In turn, Daisy felt numb. The villain might be Sugar Kane, a woman with the type of body and face that was typical of supermodels on the covers of upscale magazines. Could she have killed Kandi in a fit of anger? Anything was possible, anything at all.

Kenneth said, "I'm going to talk to Spud Gurber. I think Sugar is about to blow up."

Daisy agreed. "I was just wondering what kind of woman could continue with her life as if nothing major had happened."

Kenneth knew full well that Sugar Kane was feeling far from normal. "Her eyes are too bright, too feverish. She talks fast. The pulse at her temple is erratic. It's not a healthy situation."

Daisy crossed her arms. "I hope she doesn't have a gun or something in that big old purse she's carrying."

"So do I."

Eight

The garden show was nearly finished. News media crawled all over the place and Daisy felt as if she fought one small fire after another. All she had left to do was hand out awards within the next hour. After that, the show was over.

When she found out from Miss Myrtle and Miss Tilly that Stella and Sugar were competing to find the killer before the last award was handed out, she went in search of Kenneth to let him know what was happening. The consequences of the fight might prove deadly.

Daisy didn't make it to Kenneth's side unscathed. She spotted him talking to Spud Gurber and fell facefirst between the old roses and the hybrid teas displayed for judging and exhibition.

When she reached his side, Spud took one look at her face and told Kenneth to meet him at the podium in twenty minutes for a quick follow-up. Kenneth nodded his head in acknowledgment that he'd heard Spud, but his eyes were only for Daisy. She was coming apart at the seams.

He sat her in a tan metal folding chair near

a prize-winning grandiflora rose specimen and straddled the chair beside her. "Tell me what happened."

Daisy's face and voice were full of bewilderment. "Somebody tripped me and I pretty much skidded across the floor on my face. If it hadn't been for Whitney Webb breaking my fall, I'd have cracked my head against one of the exhibition tables."

It was 2:00 in the afternoon and the show was in its last forty minutes of production. While a muscle worked in Kenneth's jaw as he struggled to control his anger, Daisy looked around the open room to see who was doing what with whom.

Mr. Dillingsworth was deep in discussion with Stella. Sugar was prancing around under the watchful eye of Spud Gurber. Zenith had put the clean-up crew in action. Cinnamon Hartfeld was setting up the awards table with Rita in the hospitality room. Knowing that everything was under control, Daisy felt free to let it all hang out.

She said, "I can't tell you how glad I am you're here, Kenneth. I was so mad at you for stirring things up, for making me look at my friends with suspicion, but right now, I feel safer with you than I would with Spud, and I've known Spud Gurber my entire life."

Kenneth wanted to touch her, but he didn't. She was close to crying and he knew she didn't want to get completely unraveled in public. "You know that saying about everything happens for a reason. It does. I'm here because I'm supposed to be here. This way, Spud can concentrate on doing his job and I can concentrate on you."

Spud had been Daisy's protector since elementary school, and though it was hard for him to relinquish her care to someone else, he recognized that her safety was in hands as good as or better than his own.

In Kenneth, Daisy had found a champion, a role neither man had discussed beyond a handshake and a man-to-man look that required no words. The ring Kenneth placed on Daisy's finger had been sanctioned by a man who loved her the way an older brother loved his baby sister. Spud was finally able to step into the background of Daisy's life.

Daisy's unconscious mind registered the shift between Spud and Kenneth, but she didn't have the time to really think about the what and the why of their change. She just knew she was tired and in order to rest, she needed to feel safe. She felt safe with Kenneth.

He said, "Are you sure you were tripped?"

"Yes. I felt a foot on my ankle. Stella was nearby. Cinnamon. Zenith. Sugar. Mr. Dillingsworth. Mom."

Kenneth appreciated her straightforward attitude. By giving him those names, she'd narrowed down the list of suspects from a room full of people to a very select few. Every one of those people was someone she couldn't imagine as a killer. Neither could he.

He said, "Maybe Whitney Webb tripped you and tried to pretend she was helping you by redirecting your fall from the table to the ground."

Daisy found that hard to believe. "No. She was walking toward me. She couldn't have tripped me and caught me, too."

"Isn't she one of those people who was mad because vegetables were excluded from the competition?"

Daisy was impressed. "Gosh, you've got a great memory. Yes, but after we talked, she seemed okay."

A nerve twitched beneath Kenneth's left eye. "I can see by your expression that there's more you aren't telling me."

Daisy cleared her throat and said, "Well, usually when Whitney Webb holds a grudge, she doesn't let go."

He was clearly bewildered. "I don't see why anyone would want to hurt you."

"It's about as crazy as someone killing Kandi Kane. Somebody around here is completely wacko."

"Both incidents have timing in common," Kenneth said. "Kandi's killer went unnoticed in a very busy hotel. If it's true that one of those six suspects tripped you up, then that person did it in a very public place.

"If the incidents are related, then they say a lot about the killer. Number one, the person is organized, intelligent, and determined. Number two, the person is bold as hell."

Daisy caught a whiff of Kenneth's frustration and the whiff was strong. "We've ruled out Whitney Webb. Let's not narrow in on Zenith, either. I mean, she's my best girlfriend. The killer absolutely cannot be my best girlfriend."

Kenneth glared at her. "Let's not narrow it down to Sugar Kane or Stella Fitzgerald, while we're at it." He was being sarcastic.

Daisy didn't like where this conversation was headed. "Slow down, Kenneth. We're not part of any murder investigation or any other kind of investigation. The first time I met you, you were injured during the course of solving a weird crime. Back then, I was foolish enough to want to help you capture the bad guys."

"And now?"

Daisy drew in a deep breath and let it go— hard. "Now I want to do everything I can to maintain the quiet lifestyle I have. I thrive on peace and quiet, Kenneth. Let the Guthrie Police Department and whoever else that's official around here handle the case. I'm not qualified to deal with sickos."

His face was swept clean of emotion, but his eyes were hard and cold and bright. "Are you implying that I don't want a quiet life?"

Daisy grabbed the bull by the horns. "Since I've met you, Kenneth, I've discovered you work hard, you're decisive and honorable. You're attentive. The biggest quirk you have, at least in my opinion, is that you're a night owl."

"But?" he prompted, his voice low, deep, almost harsh. He didn't want to be at odds with

Daisy, and yet he was at odds and he didn't like it. The last thing they needed to be right now was at each other's throats.

She forced her breathing and stance to remain even. Thank God she'd learned how to calm herself with yoga techniques in a class she'd taken many years ago at the YMCA. "But you love action."

"And I'm a private detective."

Daisy slogged ahead to the finish line. "Right. You're either in trouble or investigating trouble."

"Don't stop now."

"I'm sorry Kandi Kane is dead. I want to know, just like everybody else, what happened to her, but I'm not starved for information. I don't want to be an amateur detective and I don't want violence in my home or at my job."

Kenneth eyed her as a stranger might study a passenger at a bus stop: assessing, remote, polite. She'd corrected her make-up and dusted herself off. She was also back in her I'm-an-independent-woman mode, Charlie's Angels-style.

He said, a little too quietly and a little bit dangerously, "Did it ever occur to you that maybe you were born to be in the thick of things?"

Daisy flung her hands in the air in disbelief. "I'm surrounded by every plant you need to make a cottage garden, one of the most classic romance gardens of all time, and you have the nerve to sit here and tell me that I was born for trouble!"

He had never seen her so thoroughly ticked off. He gentled his tone before she totally blew a gasket and told him what he could do with himself. He didn't think it would be something nice and he didn't think it mattered that she loved him or that he loved her or that the place was crawling with cops, detectives, nosy news people, and prying spectators. "That is not what I said."

Daisy wasn't in the mood to be patronized. "It may not be what you said, but it's definitely what you meant. Admit it!"

Kenneth finally understood the expression *You look beautiful when you're mad.* Daisy's eyes were clear and sparkling. Her skin had a wonderful glow and all her attention was zeroed in on him. He almost laughed at her resiliency. She was like a plant that perked up after a shot of Miracle-Gro instant plant and vegetable fertilizer.

"Calm down, Daisy, and let me explain something."

"You can explain all you want," she said, her arms crossed at the chest. "I'll calm down when I'm good and ready."

She sounded silly and pouty and was suddenly embarrassed. This man was doing everything in his power to help her keep her act together and she was taking her frustrations out on him. She wasn't being fair, and not being fair ran against her nature.

Aware of her shift in feelings, Kenneth did

laugh. Things were going to be all right. "I love it when you get ticked off."

Daisy found it hard to stay mad at him when he looked at her the way he would consider a delicious bowl of ripe berries, fruit so sweet it didn't need any sugar. "Go on, Mr. Detective. Tell me who you think I am."

"You're thirty-five, never married, no longer single since you're my"—he paused to grin lasciviously—"fiancé."

She smacked him on the arm.

"Your children are the flowers in your garden. You're an excellent Southern-style cook—when you do cook—and the only weakness I've ever noticed is your tendency to be a bleeding heart."

"I am *not* a sucker for lost causes and underdogs."

"If that wasn't true, Daisy, I wouldn't be here," he said, referring to the day she rescued him from her garden, where he'd been dumped, unconscious, beat up, and without identification. It seemed like it had happened in the ancient past, but it had hardly been a full year.

"Okay," she said, "but I'm not a sucker for every lost cause. Let's just say I've got a great eye for potential." She was referring to him.

"Ouch."

"I prefer to think I've got a strong sense of adventure," she said, her nose in the air at a haughty angle.

"Something we both have in common."

Her eyes clouded up for a second. "But you said I like to be in the thick of things—*born* is the exact word you used."

"If you'd just stay calm, I'll explain why I said what I said."

"I'm as calm as I'm gonna get," she admitted. "I just don't like knowing you think I go out looking for trouble. That's what you do as a P.I."

"I look for truth," he explained. "Period. And I don't like unsolved puzzles, but we aren't talking about me, we're talking about—"

"That's right," she said, her tone raggedy around the edges. "You're supposed to explain to me what you mean about me and trouble."

"Not trouble, Daisy. Excitement. Drama."

He ran a soothing hand from her left shoulder to her elbow, then gave her elbow a reassuring squeeze. Their impromptu conversation was reviving her.

He was glad their fight was over. "That's how I see you, Daisy. Strong. Beautiful. Courageous. Loyal. Kind. You don't look for trouble, but if it comes your way, you don't turn away from it. Neither do I."

She winked. "I suppose that's why we're such a great match."

"Yes. I can do my brand of work anywhere in the country. Guthrie is where you live and I find no reason to ask you to leave when it's so much more practical and convenient for me to come here."

The admission caused tension to fall away

from Kenneth's wide shoulders. Life was definitely good and Kandi Kane's murder reminded him about the importance of embracing joy today instead of saving it to treasure tomorrow. Tomorrow might never come. What if someone had stabbed Daisy in the crowd instead of tripping her?

Daisy's heart felt full. "You won't be sorry?"

"We both know there are no guarantees in life, only opportunities. I want this chance to be near you full-time. I want to make you a permanent part of my life, Daisy, but not my whole life. If I tried to make you my sole source of happiness, we'd both be miserable."

"I'm glad to hear you say that, Kenneth, because I was worried that once you got here and things didn't work out the way we expect and dream about, you'd blame me for your loss of happiness."

He was shaking his head before she could finish. "Grown men take responsibility for who they are and what they've done with their lives, good or bad."

"Okay. I'd say we understand each other pretty well at this point. I'm glad you've decided to stay." She could hardly wait to get home again, get out of her clothes, and into his arms. "I love you."

Kenneth's blood heated up. "We better get back into the swing of things before we get caught making out in a very public place."

"Yeah," she said. "It's time for the last round

of judging and Sugar Kane thinks she knows whodunit. She might be wrong."

"She might be in danger physically. Emotionally, she's got to be a wreck," Kenneth said. "I figure she's still in a state of shock."

"Cold rage is more like it. I'd better go find her. She doesn't want me to interfere with anything, and to tell you the truth, I don't quite know what to say to her or how to act with her. It's uncomfortable enough to carry on the show without Kandi."

Kenneth felt like the day would never end and he wouldn't get to go home with Daisy. "I've got Mr. Dillingsworth watching Sugar."

Tragic in her beauty, vulnerable in her quest, Sugar was running around questioning people without knowing who they were or how they fit into the big picture. There was no telling who meant her well and who meant her harm. She was the most likely person to be killed if the murderer wasn't finished yet.

"You're kidding?" Daisy said. "Mr. Dillingsworth? He's in his seventies. I'd hate for him to be put in the position of having to defend her. He might get hurt himself."

"He knows to contact me or Spud if he can. My goal with Sugar is to make sure she lives to stir the pot her mother left behind."

"Powerful words, Mr. Detective."

"I've had an earful about Kandi today," he said, thinking about the garden club members, each determined to give him an opinion on who they thought the killer would turn out to be. None of them suspected each other. All of them suspected Stella, who just laughed in their faces. Still, the circle of suspects had been narrowed to six. One of the six was guilty, but which one?

"I've had an earful, too," Daisy said. "I was surprised to find out so many people had come to the event because Kandi was going to be here and they wanted to meet her."

"The exhibitors aren't paying me much attention," Kenneth said, disgusted. "I'm not the police and I'm not a garden show planner. I'm about as visible as a hole in the wall. People are gawking and talking as if they're at a magic show and don't want to miss the next shocking trick. I almost wish I had a badge and a uniform."

Daisy couldn't picture him in a uniform. He looked just fine in his dark blue jeans and his short-sleeve white shirt. "Spud is all over the place, I noticed."

Kenneth grinned. "What are friends for anyway?"

Daisy wanted nothing more than to close her eyes and snuggle against Kenneth's chest. "Let's hurry up and end this thing. I wanna go home."

"Daisy!" a woman screamed, "Daisy!"

It was Rita. She ran over to Kenneth and Daisy, grabbed her daughter by the shoulders and shook her with each following word: "It's . . . Stella! She's . . . dead!"

Nine

Stella Fitzgerald was dead in the hospitality room. According to Spud Gurber, she was conked over the head in the same way as Kandi Kane. Kenneth's face was unreadable, his tone of voice harsh. "The suspect list is down to five."

Daisy wanted to cry. People often said nothing ever happened in Guthrie but this was definitely big time. "We're almost finished," she said. "Only the awards are left."

Kenneth considered what he knew. For Daisy's sake, if there was a way to salvage the last program in the show, he wanted to try. Spud was doing his best to help him. The time frame for Stella's murder was narrowed to within an hour. She'd been walking around in plain view of him, the police, everybody. The raw nerve of the killer was tremendous. Kenneth ground his back teeth in frustration.

The day was a disaster. Sugar Kane was flipping her lid. Rita was shell-shocked and staggering around as if she'd been struck herself. Mr. Dillingsworth was holding a hand to his chest as if it pained him. Cinnamon Hartfeld's arms were crossed and her teeth were chattering.

Zenith was fanning the faces of Miss Myrtle and Miss Tilly with garden show programs. Spud was standing at the podium and scanning the room as if he had X-ray vision. How dare Daisy think of handing out awards at a critical time like this? How could anyone official let her?

Daisy pretended Kenneth wasn't looking at her as if she'd suddenly turned into an alien. She knew it was unreasonable to continue with the show but she felt as if her pride was on the line, and her pride was her garden center. All her planning for this event, all her labor was becoming insignificant.

She said, "Most people don't know what happened."

Kenneth eyed her speculatively, from top to bottom.

Kenneth knew she was wrong. Everybody knew what had happened. Everybody. She wasn't even fidgeting as she coolly eyed him back, as if she had willed the madness to be gone, as if she wasn't suffering from some sort of shock-induced delusion.

She was strong, stubborn, optimistic despite the odds against salvaging something good from the fiasco she had to live through. For Kenneth, honesty was everything. He wouldn't let her pull a curtain over her eyes.

He said, "Spud knows we're down to five suspects. Your garden club members know, and with Stella's death, they aren't even standing close to each other anymore. The press is trying to get to Rita because she discovered the body.

"Spud is in the process of securing the crime scene and notifying the proper authorities to take away the body. He's being as quiet about it as he can, but unless we shut this show down, totally, Daisy, someone else might die. You."

Daisy stalked over to the empty guest table. She straightened the pens in the cups, grabbed a white towel, and cleaned the table with Windex glass cleaner.

After she cleaned the table, she threw the towel down and sat on the table's edge, her gaze directed over the whispering, chattering, want-to-see-some-blood crowd. It was definitely a mad, mad world and she was one of the nuts.

"Kenneth," she said, "this sucks."

"It does."

"There won't ever be any peace around here if this killer isn't stopped, and it has to be somebody we all know and trust, somebody with access to my business and my life at all times. To a lot of businesses and lives. We're down to Cinnamon, Sugar, Mr. Dillingsworth, Zenith, and my mom. I cannot deal with this, Kenneth. I just can't."

"You don't have any other option."

"There's always an option."

"Stella Fitzgerald and Kandi Kane were both powerful women in the media circles they used as their platform. It's more logical to me that Sugar would be killed instead of Stella. She was openly digging for information into her mother's death."

"True, but it was Stella who wanted to make a big splash in the society pages," Daisy said. "It was Stella who said she thought she knew the identity of the murderer. She just needed proof."

Kenneth said. "We've learned one thing important, and that is that the killer obviously feels there is nothing left to lose."

Daisy closed her eyes and clenched her fists. "But to kill your friends?"

Kenneth shrugged. "It's like the movie *The Talented Mr. Ripley.* The killer, Matt Damon, kept offing people he knew, even when it hurt him to do it. I think that's what's happening now. Maybe the killer is also getting a kick out of escaping exposure just in the nick of time, at least one more time."

Daisy said, "I owe it to my garden club members, my regular customers, and to myself to find out what's going on, Kenneth. Once the rubberneckers get tired of nosing around the garden shop in search of gossip, I might find myself with a decreased customer base. I rely heavily on local trade. I can't afford for the locals to stay away from my business out of fear, and they would, too, as if I was somehow contaminated by Kandi's and Stella's deaths. Responsible even."

"You'll probably lose some business, Daisy, but not all. I think that'll be true regardless of whether or not the killer or killers are caught."

"I can't afford for that to happen."

Kenneth took both her hands within his own. Her hands were cold. Her meticulously planned affair lay in ruins. She was alive to begin all over again if she had to, but the experience was something she'd never forget or ever completely understand.

There had to be a silver lining somewhere. He said, "Where are most of the exhibitors coming from for the garden show?"

"Oklahoma City, Stillwater, Norman, Crescent, and Kingfisher. Guthrie."

He offered a solution. "All I'm saying is that you can continue to advertise in those areas. Heavily initially and then, based on the kind of customers the ads bring in, make your advertising dollars more specifically targeted. Say if most of your business in a month of intense advertising comes from Kingfisher, then really go after those people until you get enough of them hooked to become regulars."

Daisy gave him an I'll-think-about-it look. "I hadn't really got that far ahead in planning, but I hear what you're saying and I'll give it some study . . . later. Right now, I need to get awards distributed and people out of here as soon as the police are done talking to them."

Kenneth was in a dilemma. Stick close to Daisy and run the risk of driving her up the wall or let her do her thing and hope she didn't get hurt or killed? So far, she'd been safe and he was thankful for this, but for how long?

The misdeeds going on around them only

served to remind him of why he loved her so much. She was charming and kind, tender and graceful. There were times when he felt words weren't necessary for understanding, only touches were needed, only kisses, hand-holding, and slow sessions of serious lovemaking.

In a short period of time, she'd become his solace and his destination. She comforted him with her loyal brand of friendship. She was the end of a sometimes lonely journey to find and keep a mate. They belonged together, always, forever. If he could only manage to keep her alive.

Daisy watched the wild play of emotions on Kenneth's face as he struggled to deal with his feelings about the drama going down at the flower show. He'd come to Guthrie for a quick getaway with his girlfriend and had found himself in the middle of a controversy, one that put them both in deadly danger as they searched for a very clever killer.

Despite everything wrong, she felt electrified. Being with Kenneth had brought light and pleasure into her life, qualities that helped her know that she was cherished, that she was protected and admired as half of a very valuable partnership.

She liked the way he handled the flower show disasters, competently and without making her feel like an idiot. As a private detective and former law officer, he knew more about crime and crime fighting than she ever would know. She didn't want to know.

She preferred to celebrate life's brighter side whenever possible, and right now she craved some serious cheering up. Kenneth was definitely a bright light and he'd captured her heart when no other man had been able to do it.

He wasn't threatened by her mental strength or her business savvy. He wasn't intent on dominating her personality in order to boost his own. He understood she had priorities before she met him that would remain priorities until she was ready to relinquish them, if she was ever ready. Her chief priority was the continued success of her garden shop.

She expected more than love from him; she expected loyalty. In turn, she felt safe and justified in meeting and matching those qualities inside the closed circle of their expanding relationship.

She was practical, reliable, emotionally sound, physically fit, and able to concentrate on her goals in order to achieve greater heights of personal and professional success. This is why the flower show meant so much to her, why she wanted the crippled show to go on.

It was the first time she'd stepped away from the safety of the garden shop to exert her power and authority outside her Guthrie community, into neighboring territory. In order to wield authority, she had to have more than power; she had to have credibility. A ruined, unfinished garden show would damage her credibility.

She'd worked too hard to allow that to happen, way too hard. That Kenneth understood this and supported her even when he sensed danger, only served to further endear him to her heart. He enhanced her positive self-image and in return, she rewarded him with her steadfast allegiance.

All Kenneth's thoughts and feelings came out in five softly spoken, deeply felt words. "I'm not leaving your side."

She was delighted with his proprietary attitude. "I love your body," she said, just as soft, just as for-your-ears-only, with the tiniest hint of the joy she felt inside. "You can guard me any time."

In the face of her trust, he felt two inches taller. He also felt a greater obligation to defend and protect her. "Great compliment," he said. "Lousy timing."

"I know. Part of me feels as if this is all a bad dream."

"I understand how you feel." He took a step closer to her. He didn't touch her, not physically, but his spirit enveloped her with every wonderful wish he ever wanted for her. He wanted to be her genie in the bottle.

She took a step, too, right into his arms He pulled her close. "I always feel better when you hold me like this. Your heart beats at the same rhythm as mine."

He laughed softly. "Depends on what I'm doing when you're listening to my heart."

She smiled. "I suppose you're right."

"Since I'm not officially involved with Stella's or Kandi's murders, I'm more flexible than I would be otherwise, and I'm not a casual on-looker. I know how to search for clues by watching and listening. Someone has seen or heard something."

"Yeah," Daisy said, "that someone was Stella."

Ten

That evening, Kenneth and Daisy returned to her house. The sun had set, but the moon was bright. Cicadas were loud in the trees. June bugs were flying at the front windows, their bodies sounding like grapes being thrown against glass. At the moment, the mockingbirds were silent.

Relaxing in the living room, they kicked back on the couch with their bare feet propped up on the coffee table. They had both showered and changed into fresh clothes. It felt marvelous to be home.

Kenneth wore loose, soft knit pajama pants in navy and a ribbed cotton undershirt. His skin smelled of Dove soap and his hair was clean and shiny. He looked huge, his muscles rippling with the slightest movement in any direction.

Daisy wore dark purple stretch pants with a lighter purple top, its neckline scooped to reveal the top of her breasts and shoulders, which were creamy and smooth from the whipped cocoa butter she favored. Her hair was swept up into a loose French roll, a few tendrils escaping the pins she'd used to hold it together.

They were sitting side by side, very close, although they weren't yet touching. There was no music. They were drinking Seattle's Best Coffee from D.G.'s. The aroma of the coffee smelled heavenly and rich, its shot of caffeine invigorating to them both, especially after they'd washed away the grime accumulated at the fairgrounds.

After rotating his thick shoulders until they cracked with a little tension relief, Kenneth said, "Let's begin with the facts."

"Okay," Daisy said. "Fact number one is that a very important person was coming to the garden show."

Kenneth nodded his head in agreement. "Kandi Kane, who also happens to be the first murder victim."

"Yes. Kandi's regional coverage of the garden show was known well in advance, beginning with the twenty garden club members," Daisy said, her manner contemplative, a slight frown on her brow.

By sorting through the facts this way, some of the horror of the murders was broken into more manageable bits. Everything was so close to home that it was difficult to be objective, let alone clearheaded enough to separate emotion and logic in order to help Kenneth be effective in his quest for truth. She was doing her best.

One thing was for certain. His visit to see her and his decision to stand by her side as she dealt with the killer hidden among the colorful array of her friends had proven how much he loved her, which wasn't something that could be measured in words but in levels of emotion and degrees of desire.

His presence had kept her from being the next target, and now he sat beside her, ready to examine the oddities of the day in retrospect, his way of hunting for the truth together, his way of protecting her from more harm, and in the process, he'd captured her heart for good. This man was definitely a keeper.

In turn, Kenneth felt rooted, defined, welcomed, appreciated. He knew he was loved, that he was needed and wanted in a relationship that put curl in his toes and made his flesh hum with energy. His love for Daisy wasn't blind, but it was definitely complete.

He took a sip of his coffee. It hadn't been sweetened with honey or sugar and it hadn't been lightened with milk or cream. The coffee was strong, black and hot, just like his woman. He was thankful they were able to have this quiet time together in order to rethink and readjust to their changed circumstances.

He said, "The unusual thing about Kandi's appearance is that when she first arrived in Guthrie, she was extremely pleasant. By all accounts, this ran against her nature."

"I agree," Daisy said as she took a sip of her own steaming dark brew.

Unlike Kenneth, her coffee had been generously sweetened with C&H Sugar. Like usual, she'd added no cream, although on the rare occasion that she did use cream, it was Carnation brand evaporated milk, something she tended to do in the evenings as a sort of dessert. Tonight, she needed the sugar to pump her up.

She said, "Fact two, then, is Kandi's odd behavior."

"Which," Kenneth said, "could have incited someone to kill her. Maybe someone Kandi knew went to her hotel to confront her, only to be further outraged by her unusually pleasant behavior. That person could have been Stella, but the police don't think there are two killers. Therefore, we can rule Stella out as a suspect in both murders."

"Uh-huh," Daisy said. "The first murder might have happened because the killer might have been prepped for a fight, but when one didn't happen because Kandi was set on smooth and in a good mood, all that adrenaline went into overdrive and she got whacked over the head."

"Exactly."

Daisy rubbed her aching temples with the pads of her fingertips, then took several sips of coffee and hoped the caffeine would destroy her headache. It felt as if she had a doozy coming on. "This leads us to fact three: Stella's death."

"Her murder."

"And your conclusion?" Daisy asked.

Stella's death had hit harder than Kandi's because she'd known Stella longer and better and she'd seen her less than an hour before she was murdered. Daisy had a hard time saying murder and Stella in the same sentence.

Whenever she even thought about the two words together, her head throbbed. It throbbed because the truth about whodunit and why was going to be painful and revealing. In this case, friends were killing friends.

"My conclusion," Kenneth said, "is that a killer is right here staring us in the face, so to speak, and you know who the person is, which only adds to your own feelings of weirdness. The same is true for everybody else involved in this case who happen to know both victims. According to Spud Gurber earlier today, both Kandi and Stella had no defense wounds. This is significant enough to be noted as fact four."

"Okay," Daisy said, "this means that the killer is also known by the local officials, at least around Guthrie. We know this because no one claims to have seen or heard anything unusual, even after extensive interviews by the police and even by the news people—by the way, you did a great job keeping them away from me—"

"No problem. I was glad I was on hand to do it."

"It wasn't easy, either," Daisy said. "In a small town like this one, strangers are noticed quick and you aren't known by a lot of people yet. You acted official but you didn't have a uniform or a badge and there were some folks questioning your authority to tell them what to do. I heard a few of the grumbles.

"Around here, people want to know where you're from, why you're in town, how long you'll be staying, where you're staying, who you've visited already, what time you're leaving to go back home, and when you think you'll be back to town for another visit."

Kenneth laughed. He'd been asked those same questions on more than one occasion since coming to visit. Now that most people knew he was visiting with Daisy, they left him alone other than to ask how long he'd be staying this time around or when he was planning to do the right thing and marry that girl.

"Maybe," he said. "In my work experience, people tend to see and hear or sense more than they realize. Kandi had previous connections to Guthrie through her daughter. Those connections tie to you, as well. Sugar Kane went to school here. Chester Whitcomb went to school with Sugar and had worked with you."

"Well, if you go that route, then you have to say Stella Fitzgerald and my mom are connected."

"True."

Daisy went on as if she hadn't heard him. "Kandi died from a bashed skull. Stella died the same way. Bashed skull. I guess," she said, almost to herself, "that's another connection. Kind of like pairs of circles within circles. Everything is connected. Everything is up close. Everything is hard to deal with. Everything is happening too fast. Everything feels like TV, like all I have to do is press the off button on the tube and my little world will be what it's supposed to be all over again: normal and safe."

Kenneth knew full well this was a woman in the throes of denial. Instead of stating the obvious, he chose a neither-here-nor-there approach. "Kind of."

"This is terrible," Daisy said as she stared at coffee grounds at the bottom of her mug. "I mean, the few details I do know are revolting. Real blood and real guts and true insanity. I feel like going home to get away from it all, only I am at home."

The last three words came out as a plaintive wail. At that precise moment Daisy wasn't trying to be strong, she wasn't trying to act tough and I-can-handle-whatever-gets-dished. She was letting all her insecurities out on the table for a judicious airing.

At home, there was usually a great aura of tranquillity around her but no matter how hard she wished it to happen, her life would never feel as comfortable as it had before Kandi's life was snuffed out by somebody she knew, somebody she trusted like a relative or an old and dear friend. Daisy's trust in all things familiar had been violated.

"Fact five," she said, "is that we're down to four suspects: Cinnamon, Mr. Dillingsworth, Zenith, and my mom. Sugar was arguing with Spud at the time of Stella's murder. She was telling Spud she wanted all the suspects taken to jail for questioning and he told her that she was one of the suspects. That's why they were arguing. Sugar couldn't believe anybody could think she'd killed her own mother. She was incensed."

Kenneth went in the kitchen to refill their coffee mugs. After he returned to the living room he said, "While you were wrapping things up at the fairgrounds, I had a talk with Spud and other authorities. There was a note left at the second crime scene."

Daisy's laugh was rough and reckless. Her eyes were wide. She looked as nutty as she sounded. "And I didn't think this mess could get any worse." She felt a migraine coming on for sure.

Kenneth eyed her with care but he knew she was more stable than she appeared. She wasn't hiding under the blankets the way she clearly wanted to be. Only cowards stepped away from the plate and Daisy was definitely not a coward.

He said, "The note was one of those old-fashioned magazine cut-out things on plain white paper. The kind you might see used as a ransom note on a television movie."

"Tell me what it said." Her voice was filled with all the dread she would feel if someone had asked her to hold a live snake: choked and low pitched.

"The note said: 'The first was a bitch. The second was a bad penny.'

Daisy shuddered. "That's awful."

"The note wasn't signed," Kenneth explained. "The police are having it processed for clues."

"So," Daisy said, "we need to keep approaching this problem by the steady elimination of suspects."

"It's working."

Daisy grimaced. She just couldn't wrap her mind around the facts, couldn't digest them, couldn't look them head on, but she had to do it. She couldn't let the killer go free. "We've got my mom, my childhood friends, and a senior citizen."

"We're gonna get through this, Daisy."

On a piece of lined paper, Kenneth formalized the list. The paper read:

1. Zenith Braxton: Miniature-rose buff, she swears the top prize would have belonged to her if she'd been allowed to participate in the show
2. Mr. Dillingsworth: One of Daisy's best customers and Zenith's gardening rival
3. Cinnamon Hartfeld: She likes to dig for secrets and then spread the news
4. Rita Rogers: Daisy's mother; she was the queen of discretion until Stella started taunting her in front of the Masonic Temple

Daisy couldn't think of anyone else that needed to go on the list. She said, "I think we need to tackle this problem cold-bloodedly."

"Right," Kenneth said, then tapped the top of his pen against his chin. "Since we aren't able to visit the crime scenes, we must rely on the evidence presented to us by Spud Gurber.

We also need to use the evidence we collected based on personal observations. What we're doing now."

"As in what we saw or heard that might prove whodunit?"

He stopped bouncing the pen against his chin to look at her. "Yeah."

Daisy stared at him in admiration. He made her feel like she knew what she was doing. She said, "Zenith and Cinnamon had full access to everything and so their presence in any given area would not be questioned. Same thing goes with Mom. She could have done it, even Mr. Dillingsworth could have done it, I suppose. They just don't compute. One is too kind and the other is too old. That leaves Zenith or Cinnamon. It can't be Zenith or Cinnamon."

Kenneth covered her fidgety hands with both of his own. "Your mother had an alibi for the first murder. We think there is only one killer. I think that leaves Zenith, Cinnamon, and Mr. Dillingsworth."

Daisy shuddered with distaste, then took another sip of coffee to bolster her nerves. "Either suspect is awful."

Kenneth said, "As bad as that sounds and as bad as it hurts, honesty and clear thinking could mean the difference between catching a killer or letting one go because feelings might get hurt."

Daisy took a deep cleansing breath. "Okay. What next?"

"Let's view the evidence based on what we know about chronological events."

She squared up her shoulders and placed her empty mug on the table with a decisive thunk. "Okay. Shoot."

"In March of this year, you and the garden club decided to run a flower show and exhibition in Guthrie."

"Yes," Daisy said. "The idea is to make the show an annual event if possible. If the show gets too large to be held at the fairgrounds, we'll try to move it to Oklahoma City. That way, we'll have access to bigger facilities. We'll decide where we'll have it during a planning committee."

Kenneth made notes on paper. "So, it's reasonable to say that the competitive nature of some of the contestants may have gotten out of hand."

Daisy made a face. "No. The victims were not participants."

"I disagree," Kenneth said. "Kandi Kane and Stella Fitzgerald were reporters, but they were also judging the entire event in order to write about it. This means their individual tastes and preferences would influence the stories they'd write. It's possible that an exhibitor wanted a special angle done, which both Kandi and Stella refused to do. My point is that we could be wrong about the suspects. Remote as it is, the chance exists."

Daisy's face clearly said she thought Kenneth was way off track with that line of thinking.

"The only way I can make your idea fit is the fact that both Kandi and Stella were actually gardeners. You saw from Stella's yard she was really into her gardening hobby. Also, Kandi was actually a farm girl. I've heard that at one time her gardens were the size of small crops."

Kenneth considered this new information. "Okay, what this tells me is that both women were not superficially involved in this event."

Daisy knew where he was headed. "I keep telling you that. Both women were as fanatical about flowers for gardening and exhibition as the rest of us, but that's the extent of their action. Kandi was a farm girl who portrayed the high life in her professional work. She was glamorous and well-spoken.

"On the other, but related, hand, Stella wanted to report about society living, and yet she couldn't get away from her old-fashioned country girl roots any more than Kandi could. The women clashed and melded in a way that made them enemies of each other. We've got the suspects right.

"Stella had dirt on Kandi but she ended up looking for Kandi's killer. When she found out who it was, the killer murdered her, too. Physical evidence suggests Kandi knew the killer, as well. I think it's someone Kandi knew from the past that Stella knew in the present."

Kenneth smiled. "You didn't want to be an amateur detective, but you've just done your first bit of deducting. We're establishing evidence pretty quickly and efficiently. Clues and answers to clues are stacking up rather nicely."

Daisy was beginning to feel the same way. "The entire process is strange, but it's also comforting. It makes me feel useful rather than helpless."

Kenneth put the pen down and drew her into his arms. "Murder is painful business while it's happening and a constant nightmare for the living. Killing someone is always about a loss of control and an inability to connect emotionally to other people. This is why I'm so serious about making our relationship together work. Good things should be cherished. What we have is a good thing."

Daisy frowned. "Are you saying you want to be with me in order to stay connected to people?"

"No. I'm saying that I've learned life is good and that being in love makes life beautiful. You make me feel brand-new every day that I'm with you. I feel as if nothing can stop me, that everything I ever dreamed of can come true. I can have property in Guthrie, something I always wanted. I can have a woman who loves me as much as I love her. I can have peace here. Respect.

"I like the open spaces and lack of congestion. I like the way people say hello, just because. I like taking the time to talk to the cashier and the people in line while I'm in the store making a purchase."

Daisy laughed. "I guess people around here are pretty nosey."

His smile was genuine. "Yes, but it feels good to be noticed. It's nice to have people take time to find out what I've been up to, to talk about politics and sports and the weather and really know that what I say matters. I like the sense of balance I feel when I'm in Guthrie and the best part about it is that it's independent of you. What I feel for you, being with you, that makes relocating a smooth transition. Kind of like icing on a perfect cake."

Daisy wasn't sure if she should be miffed or not about what he'd just said. She poked him in the arm. "Gee, thanks."

He kissed her on the forehead. "No. Thank you."

Gently, she pushed him on the thigh; then she scooted over closer so that they were touching shoulder to shoulder. "If we start kissing and stuff we'll end up making love on the sofa."

His grin was lecherous. "Sounds good to me."

She poked him again, harder this time. "But we need to get on with this evidence-gathering business, so we can find out what happened to Kandi and Stella. I won't be able to rest until their killer is caught."

Kenneth knew she was right. "Okay. I arrived here on Saturday afternoon for a two-week vacation with you. The plan was for me to spend the first week helping you prepare for and run the flower show and then spend the second week of vacation helping you relax after the show."

"Right. So the killer, whom we presume is known to us, also knew that you'd be on hand at the show. Even though you aren't the police, you're definitely an authority figure. Having you at the show, watching you with me, must have added a sense of danger and thrill to the killer's actions. Like the killer in *The Talented Mr. Ripley.*"

Kenneth nodded his head in agreement. "I've been thinking the same thing. I think this person feels smarter than all of us. Why else do it so up close and personal? Kandi's death happened in a hotel, but it was right at the time she should have been on her way to Guthrie to speak."

"Are you thinking of someone introverted as the killer?" Daisy asked.

Kenneth reached over to a side table and flicked a light on. The living room took on a warm glow that had the soothing effect of candlelight. "What do you mean?"

"Kandi and Stella were outspoken and knowledgeable. Maybe the killer was conservative but felt more superior and killed them to rule out competition on that level. I just feel like their deaths aren't related to the garden show. With the exception of the sabotaged podium and two chairs, the event itself wasn't touched, just two of the key players."

"Or maybe the killer just wanted to shut them up."

"Crude way of putting it," Daisy said, "but yeah, I could see that happening. Neither Kandi or Stella were good listeners. They always knew more than the average Joe Blow. Always. It's what ticked Mom off about them."

"What else?"

"We think the killer had a problem in the past with Kandi. Maybe the killer confronted her and killed her in frustration, but it's also possible that Kandi sought the killer out and invited the person to her hotel.

"Maybe she started all the ruckus, maybe her good behavior at my place was the calm before the storm. Maybe Stella just happened to luck on something juicy simply because she was looking for a way to break into society journalism. Maybe when she mentioned to Mom at the Sandstone Cottage that she knew something, the killer heard about it and got nervous."

"Maybe."

Kenneth let her talk. In real life, all the loose ends didn't get tied. Some aspects of the case might never be explained. Murder wasn't a rational act, at least not in this case. When it was all said and done, there were bound to be a lot of questions left unanswered.

"Yeah," Daisy said, "maybe."

Kenneth met her stare with an intelligent look. He was dark and dangerous in her jewel-colored living room. He was a magician, pulling facts from her mind like bunnies from a hat. He did it in a laid-back style that kept her from feeling interrogated. He was in control but she didn't feel dominated.

He was a magnet, a man able to attract the truth and repel the lies going on around him with the ease of a modern-day Superman. His influence on her life was strong, because as re-pelled as she was by the true nature of his work—digging for clues among the ruins of murder and other less critical crimes—she was also attracted to him on purely mental and physical levels, instinctive levels that had very little to do with logic and everything to do with emotion. It was tough to keep the two separated during their behind-the-scenes investigation.

Kenneth used his analytical thinking skills to restore order, and action to enforce it; and be-cause of this, Daisy was able to respect and not fear him. He was a man who was also a friend and this friendship bound them together for all time.

Above all, he was a meditation to her, a man who listened, who reasoned, a man who lived his dreams and made room for her to live hers. He made room by not telling her how to do what she wanted to do, by not forcing his will and decisions upon her, by accepting her as the woman she chose to be rather than the woman he wanted her to be.

He saw her as an asset and not a liability or a nuisance. She would never be his "little woman," and when he did something for her, it wouldn't be a "honey do," it would be because he loved her and wanted to make her happy.

That's why he'd agreed to build props and move things around and do whatever was necessary to help her first garden show be as successful as possible. It was why she wanted to help him solve Kandi and Stella's murders when all she wanted to do was jump in the bed and hide until her world was made right again.

She leaned over and kissed him, her touch light and almost innocent, but the glow in her eyes told him that she loved him as much as she loved herself. She hadn't realized how alone she'd been until he came along and made a place for himself inside her life.

He was too strong and masculine to ever play second fiddle to her wants and needs, but he was secure enough to understand that there was room for them both to be strong in a relationship that grew more rich and satisfying everyday of their lives.

She felt they made a solid couple because they actually enjoyed being together in a way that meant they didn't have to talk to fill the silence with words or with action. In this manner, they were able to take notice and treasure the love each had for the other, and cherish the differences between them.

She squeezed his hand; it was hard and callused and a little scratchy. He'd been moving roses around without gloves and the thorns had marked his skin. He'd told her that real men didn't wear gardening gloves and she'd laughed.

She figured he'd get tired of being scratched soon enough. Gloves kept dirt from getting under fingernails and kept the red Guthrie soil from staining the skin, kept insects from biting and kept nicked flesh on the minimum. He'd learn the hard way, but learn he would.

Noticing her melancholy mood shift to a lighter one, Kenneth felt a wave of desire move through his body, the bulk of it settling between his thighs. She was sexy without trying to be sexy. Her lashes were dark and shiny. Her lips were full and soft. Her skin glowed with health and when she spoke, her voice had that come-hither note that never failed to turn him on.

She said, "Wanna play connect the dots?"

Instantly, his mind formed a picture of the ebony-colored mole on her ankle. He pictured each mole along the way from her ankle to her right shoulder. His smile, rueful and tight, expressed very eloquently his sorrow: he wanted to play with her, but resolution of the murders was imperative. He had to stick to the gathering of much-needed evidence.

He said, "Let's finish what we were doing and then we can relax. I want to get this information over to Spud as soon as possible."

Not surprised by his line of thinking, Daisy pulled him closer and spoke in his ear. "I don't figure I've told you lately that I love it when you talk dirty."

"Woman," he said with feeling, "you're too much."

She winked. "Thank you."

"When all this is over," he promised, "I'm going to lock you up in the bedroom until we have to eat real food or die."

Her laugh was hot and throaty. "Sounds good to me."

Kenneth was glad she was such a winner. Her nights had been sleepless and her days had been filled with worry about something going wrong with the show that she wouldn't be able to fix—and it had gone wrong and she hadn't been able to fix it: nobody could.

Nothing was turning out right, despite all the planning she and her friends had done to make the garden show a spectacular event. The show was memorable, but not for the right reasons.

Kenneth hauled her to her feet and moved off to the kitchen. He took two fresh mugs from the cupboard. They were the dark green mugs with her business logo set on a cream-colored square. The square was adorned with a trio of cabbage roses held together with ribbon. The image was down-to-earth, practical and elegant, just like Daisy, even during stressful times such as these.

From the refrigerator, Kenneth took out the Tupperware pitcher marked ICED COFFEE. It was coffee-flavored with melted vanilla ice cream and Italian syrup. Today's syrup was caramel. Daisy had been liberal with the syrup and so the iced coffee was incredibly rich, and incredibly sweet. He downed the cold concoction in a flash, smacked his lips, and poured himself another.

Daisy laughed. "I'll turn you into a coffee junkie for real if you stick around me long enough."

He licked more cream off his lips. "I'm sticking."

She downed her drink and poured herself a fresh cup. "Damn, that's good."

The quicker they got back to business, the quicker they'd be able to dally together between the bedsheets. He sat down at the kitchen table. "I want to review the garden club."

"Okay. Shoot."

"Tell me again how many members you have in the club."

Her response was instant. "Twenty. Meetings usually have about half the club roster in attendance. It's an informal gathering that often begins and ends with me ringing up sales on the register."

Kenneth narrowed his focus. "Tell me about Cinnamon Hartfeld."

Daisy brought her friend up to mind. Cinnamon was petite and trim after a diet that cut fifteen pounds off her formerly plump figure. She ran an antique store on Harrison Street.

"She hates secrets and is generally known as a pleasant little busybody. She's at every chamber coffee and she's on several festival planning committees. Cinnamon makes it her business to keep up with Who's Who in Guthrie."

"Kandi's unusual behavior would have intrigued her then," Kenneth said, referring to

Kandi's friendly attitude the first day she arrived in Guthrie, an attitude that was considered atypical by everyone who'd run into her that day.

"Yes, but I can't visualize Cinnamon as a heartless killer."

"But you agree that the killer has to be someone you know? Someone close to you, the speakers, the media, the event." This was not a question. He kept bringing it up because he didn't want her to relax her guard with anyone until she figured out who had it in for Kandi and Stella.

"Yes."

"Then Cinnamon Hartfeld is a viable suspect for murder." He spoke with force, that cold light back in his eye again. There would be no sugar-coated words from Kenneth when it came to examining evidence.

Daisy smacked her hand on the kitchen table. "This sucks."

"Tell me about Zenith's connection."

Daisy knew Zenith was on his suspect list but she was still appalled to even think of her friend as a criminal. "She wouldn't hurt a fly."

Kenneth's look and tone were blunt. "I've been in her company four times since I've met you and each time she needled the heck out of you. Zenith Braxton likes to get on people's nerves."

"But she's harmless," Daisy argued.

"She's a suspect."

"She would never approach Kandi to needle

her because she wouldn't want to run the risk of Kandi writing something nasty about her."

Kenneth drummed a short tattoo on the tabletop. "I agree, but it's not Kandi I'm thinking about. I'm thinking of Stella."

Daisy sucked in a short, sharp breath, then let it go with a quick woosh. "Zenith hated Stella's guts. How'd you guess?"

"Zenith looked like she wanted to spit on Stella whenever she did bother to look at her. I figured that it was out of loyalty to you that she didn't. Did she think Stella broke your parents up?"

Daisy swung her eyes over him as if he really was a magician and she was trying to figure out one of his tricks. "How'd you guess?"

"I remember you said that you and Zenith have a long-standing rivalry together but that you were raised close enough to be sisters. She might needle you but she admires you. If she killed Stella, she might have done so out of information she learned from Cinnamon who *would* have been bold enough to approach Kandi."

Daisy pursed her lips and nodded her head no. She said staunchly, "Zenith is not the killer."

"It's somebody I trust, too, if that makes you feel any better."

Daisy paced the kitchen and then stopped in front of him. She slapped her hands on her hips. She did it hard enough to make Kenneth think she wanted to slap him for constantly repeating that one of her friends was a criminal. "I know these people!"

"I know you, too, but I think that even you would kill for the right reasons."

"No reason is right."

Kenneth knew better and so did she. He said, "Self-defense."

Frustrated, Daisy walked away.

He followed her. "Where are you going?"

"The backyard."

"Ahh," Kenneth said, "your sanctuary."

"Yes."

Outside, Daisy flung each foot in the air so that her rubber clogs went flying across the patio. She needed the comforting ritual of working in her garden. What better way than to yank weeds from the flower beds?

Behind her, Kenneth flicked on the patio lights. No woman in her right mind would pull weeds at this hour, but then, Daisy was no ordinary woman, and even in the half-light she could tell the difference between a weed and a flower.

Her behavior made as much sense to him as Stella and Rita having a singing match, which had turned out to be the last one they'd ever have. It was *Twilight Zone* to the max in Guthrie tonight.

Content to leave her alone for the moment, he used the opportunity to unwind a notch. He slipped a jazz disc into the portable stereo on the patio table, sat in a chair, legs stretched out in front of him, and watched Daisy's butt sway as she set about yanking weeds. If he thought she'd let him make love to her, he'd lie down beside her, but he knew that now wasn't a good time. Right now, she needed to think. They both did.

As usual, Cutie Pie relaxed in a corner, but she wasn't sleeping. She watched the two of them, her face resting on her paws, tail softly switching from side to side as she acknowledged that Kenneth was as aware of her as she was of him. The dog had grown to welcome and love him, but her first loyalty would always be to Daisy.

Daisy found as much comfort in Cutie Pie as she did in her garden as she quietly, diligently made a short stack of weeds: hen bit, lamb's quarters, and that ever ruthless quack grass, plus one volunteer elm tree that was only four inches tall.

Four, she thought.

The final number of suspects.

As she worked, Daisy registered the watchful, waiting attitude Kenneth portrayed. He was edgy but alert, and she knew from experience that he was evaluating the events that had taken place this day.

It was hard to believe he'd been there almost a week. From start to finish, nothing had been easy since his arrival. Yet from the beginning, Kenneth had been constant, vigilant, a comfort and a friend.

As she had been when he first stepped off the plane and into her arms, Daisy was electri-

fied with energy. Her nerves were excited and
her stomach was jumpy, which is why she was
trying to calm herself in the garden, even
though it was almost too dark to see and the
bugs were biting because she'd forgotten to
spray herself with insect repellent.

When it got down to it, Kenneth was as devoted to his work as he was to her and even
though he wasn't an official investigator in the
flower show murders, he was acting as if he was.
She was getting to see the man in action.

This meant she couldn't pretend, even for a
little while, that everything was going to be all
right, that Kandi and Stella weren't just pulling
some kind of sick prank, that they really were
alive somewhere, not conked over the head in
a fit of rage or jealousy or something as equally
sinister by the hand of a common enemy.

Daisy had secretly feared that she would fail
the garden show and she had: something ugly
had happened and that ugly thing would always
be connected to future exhibitions. Kenneth
was doing his best to salvage what was left of
her pride, and she welcomed the help even
though she hated the method he had to use in
order to get the job done: bold questioning and
constant note taking.

When Daisy felt calm enough to stop yanking
weeds, she dusted off her hands and knees and
sat with Kenneth at the patio table. Cutie Pie,
ever in tune with her mistress's moods, had
changed from her position to lay at Daisy's feet.

Kenneth reached down to scratch the shepherd behind the ears. The dog groaned with pleasure and rolled over so that her head rested on the slope of Daisy's bare right foot. "Between me and Cutie Pie, you're pretty well protected tonight."

She sighed softly. "I know."

After a long, rather companionable silence, she said, "When I started this thing, I knew that a good word from Kandi would boost my sales. It did, but it wasn't what she said that made the difference, it was her getting killed. I don't have enough inventory left to warrant opening the shop until Monday. I'm going to close for the rest of next week and just spend time with you. I've never run out of inventory, Kenneth."

"When you open again, let people know I'll be designing yard follies," Kenneth suggested. He was beginning to feel the same excitement about the joint project as she was. He was ready to get started, ready to move on with the rest of their life together.

"People will love it," she said. "Thank you."

Kenneth's love for Daisy was clear in his voice and in his body language. There was a subtle softening just beneath his normal tough exterior. "You're welcome. The week break in your business will give us time to figure out how to present the idea to your public."

"True."

After three beats of silence, he said, "Are you ready to talk about Stella?"

Her heart was racing again. "I guess. Every

time I think about her, I feel the way I do when I drink espresso."

Kenneth rocked a brow up a notch at her pointed description. "As in skin crawling with the willies?"

She nodded her head vigorously. "Yes."

"Then let's talk about Sugar Kane first."

Daisy was thankful for the reprieve. "I'd have changed my name as soon as I was grown. Sugar Kane. That's worse than being named after a flower the way I am."

"Oh, I don't know," he said. "I couldn't imagine you with any other name besides the one you've got. Even though you grow roses for a living, you don't look like a Rose."

"Gee, thanks."

"You know what I mean."

She let him off the hook. "Yeah, I do. I'm a little too feisty to be a Rose."

"Exactly."

She punched him in the arm. His bicep felt like a rock. "Anyway, once upon a time, Sugar was a college student at Langston. While there, she met Chester Whitcomb. Unfortunately, Chester turned out to be a serious bad guy, a prescription drug dealer who also got tangled up in a murder investigation."

"I know the rest. It's also because of Chester Whitcomb that I met you," Kenneth said.

"Wouldn't it be strange," Daisy said, "if Kandi's death was somehow related to Chester? I mean, think about it. So much of who we are as people is tied up in the past. Gossip has it that Kandi ran away from her past as a country girl to build a life as a society figure. Maybe she hadn't made a good choice. Maybe that's why she was so mean."

Kenneth took a deep breath and released it. "She wasn't mean when she visited you here. We've got to keep that in mind."

"No. Maybe she had somehow made peace with her past."

Kenneth shook his head. All this talk of peace made him wonder why so many people seemed to look for love in all the wrong places. The right place to look for love was in the heart.

He said, "This is all speculation. We have to keep dealing with evidence. Evidence is her pleasant attitude when she arrived in Guthrie. This we know for a fact because we witnessed it firsthand when she came to the house. What led to her mean attitude prior to her getting here is totally unknown to us."

"Okay," Daisy said. "That's a fair thing to say, but I still believe that we can't get away from whatever destiny has in store for us. We can slow it down, we can run, but we can't hide from it. That could cause frustration and frustration could have prompted a rational person to do something irrational, like whacking somebody over the head."

Kenneth could have gone with that idea for the first murder but not the second one. "Was Kandi married?"

"No. While she was pregnant, Kandi busted

her husband for having sex with a woman named Bootsie. A stripper."

"Did Kandi tell you this?"

"No. Cinnamon did."

Kenneth's estimation of Cinnamon's gossip-sleuthing powers ran up a level. If what she said was true, he doubted Kandi would want the general public to know about it, especially if she'd been working so hard to separate herself from her past. "How did your friend find out something so . . . private?"

No matter how Daisy wracked her brains, she couldn't remember. She felt the same sort of mild fluster she did when she couldn't remember the title of a song, even when she knew the words and the artist. "You'll have to ask Cinnamon."

"I will." Kenneth made a note on the paper he'd retrieved from the living room while Daisy was busy yanking weeds. One half of the paper was set aside for evidence. The other half was set aside for questions. His list of questions was growing.

"Okay," Daisy said, "you arrived on Saturday. Kandi showed up on Sunday, presumably to spend time with her daughter and to relax. We know that Guthrie is billed as a great place to antique and whatever, so this would have been a great idea."

"True."

"That brings us to Monday," Daisy said. "On Monday, Mom told you about a house she wants you to see."

"She did, but we're focusing on what she said

about the flower show and Kandi Kane specifically. Forget the house. For now, anyway."

"Man, there are lots of distractions. I see why you need that paper. It keeps you on track."

Kenneth cleared his throat. "Back to Kandi Kane. When I told you I'd run into Miss Myrtle and Miss Tilly at Gus' Liquor Store to buy wine, I also told you they'd heard Kandi took a bribe to rig a sure winner."

Daisy had a no-way-in-hell look on her face. "Now, that might have been true as a rumor, but fact is, Kandi had no influence in who would win an award in any division. She was there to report on the event in general. Period. She might have accepted a bribe, but not for rigging the show for a winner."

"I hear you," Kenneth said, "but usually, there's a little bit of truth in every rumor. Tell me what could have happened."

"Well, I'd say it was more likely that Kandi was being paid hush money rather than bribe money."

Kenneth fired off a quick question. "What did she value?"

"Respectability."

Kenneth didn't think so, but he figured they were close. "She was mean, remember. It couldn't be respectability, unless . . . unless . . ."

She wasn't in the mood for more suspense. She didn't think she'd watch a mystery film or read a mystery book ever again. "Spit it out, Kenneth."

"Unless it had to do with her daughter."

Eleven

They were back in the living room. All the dishes had been cleared away. All the lamps were lit. The notes were on the coffee table. This was a think session. They were just planning to brainstorm.

Daisy said, "You can't be for real . . . about Sugar, I mean?"

"I am."

She frowned. "Why?"

Kenneth explained. "I was thinking about something Rita said. She said that 'In gardening, there are no guarantees.' "

Daisy gave him a no-kidding-Sherlock look. Anybody who'd ever dealt with the red clay soil in Guthrie knew that notion as a fact. The ground dried out on top and stayed wet on the bottom. It got hard and broke surface roots on plants, and when it rained, water ran off the top like it was going down a slippery slide.

On slopes, the red clay turned to sand and rock, but the sweet satisfaction of getting flowers to not just grow but thrive in Guthrie's compacted soil was as addicting to Daisy as the caffeine in her coffee. She thrived on gardening, coffee, close friendships, and Kenneth's love.

"Mom is correct," she said. "There aren't any guarantees."

"That applies to friendships, as well," Kenneth said. "Remember, you told me that 'In the end, the cheater would never live down the scandal if word of foul play came to light.' "

"Hey," Daisy said, "I think I know where you're headed. Just replace the word *cheater* for the word *killer.*"

Kenneth gave Daisy a now-you've-got-me look. His heavenly smile was crooked, his dark eyes were delighted. Being on track with the woman he loved gave him a powerful feeling that set him on top of the world.

He felt no crime was unsolvable and that the future they saw for themselves was a destiny they could shape with their own wills and their own minds. All they had to do was work together. "That brings us back to the issue of respectability."

Daisy almost threw her hand out for a high-five. Kenneth was running full speed in detective mode. He spoke as if his mind was a tape recorder and she was the blank tape: his sounding board.

She hadn't realized until now that when people talked, this man really listened, she really listened. Even though he was idle, his mind never truly rested. He just tended to look as if he was shooting the breeze, as he'd done while listening to jazz on the patio while she yanked up weeds from the flower beds. "Go on."

Kenneth singled out more evidence. "Your mom said Kandi was 'a regular little bitch' in Wal-Mart."

"That's right," Daisy said, her mind racing back to the conversation. "Kandi threw a temper tantrum because she didn't want to wait around like an Oakie."

Kenneth spoke with cool deliberation: Clue by clue. Point for point. "This happened after Kandi left your place. We know that when she left here, she was happy. What if she ran into somebody at Wal-Mart that shocked her out of her quiet mood and made her act like her usual old grumpy self?"

"I'm with you," Daisy said. "You're thinking that when Kandi used the word *Oakie,* she was reaching back to her farm girl roots. Her response was involuntary: anger. I say this because she was here on a professional, high-profile mission and she'd want to protect her image and credibility, which is exactly what she'd been doing until she got to Wal-Mart.

"People interested in the show would have been looking around to spot her, and so it would have been important for her to be social. If she was rude all the time, she wouldn't have been able to conduct business. Since Wal-Mart is the biggest store in town, she was likely to show up there at some point, especially since Sugar was staying here. Maybe the person who ticked Kandi off followed her there just to see what her reaction would be in a neutral zone. Wal-Mart would definitely be neutral and therefore safe."

"Right," Kenneth said. "That means we can narrow our suspects even further. We can look for someone who knew Kandi in her hometown or knew about something that Kandi would still find embarrassing today, something that happened in her past. Something Kandi might not have wanted Sugar to know."

Daisy sat up straight and snapped her fingers. "Like the way her husband cheated on her. This sent her running from her hometown."

"Right. Also, Rita reported that Sugar told her mother she 'ought to be used to Wally World by now.' "

Daisy nodded her head sagely. She was learning an awful lot about Kenneth this week. For instance, she finally saw how he could be so hooked on this detective stuff and not want to give it up completely in order to make garden furniture and other whatnots.

It was like shifting through a thousand and one puzzle pieces until the right ones snapped into place. Who didn't like a good puzzle? she figured. It was why murder-mystery themes were so popular at restaurants and hotels and in the arts.

Like most people she knew, Daisy usually liked a good mystery, especially when it was served up with a serious dose of romance. In this case, there was no gory blood to deal with firsthand. There was nothing technical to make her stomach lurch and her mind cringe, like gritty crime scene details or graphic words between homicide detectives and crime scene techs. She just needed a break from mysteries, now that her friends were involved in a real live one.

She didn't want to know what was in the mind of a killer and she wasn't willing to find out.

She and Kenneth weren't in a hurry to get anywhere: they had already arrived at their destination and their destination was love, the ultimate commitment between a man and a woman. This commitment had nothing to do with paper and everything to do with honesty, integrity, the good and the true.

This amateur sleuthing with a professional detective was strictly armchair cozy stuff for Daisy and she didn't want it to go any further than this. Until now, she never knew words and conversations could be used as evidence; but Kenneth was right, what people said and did were important.

Otherwise he wouldn't be spending his time trying to figure out the last moments of Kandi Kane's life. By centering on Kandi, he'd also help the police find out who killed Stella Fitzgerald. In order to get close enough to knock Stella down and kill her, the murderer had to be someone so benign that even she was caught off guard; knowing who the killer was, she'd allowed herself to be murdered.

Daisy spoke, a little bit of anger over the entire situation thrown into her tone. " 'Used to it' as in common Oakies. Common country folk behavior." She hated those terms and the negative attitude that usually came from the people who said such things.

In Daisy's experience, people brought up in largely rural backgrounds were very protective of family and friends, the reason she was having such a hard time believing anybody she knew was a selfish, opportunistic murderer, which is exactly how she felt about the killer.

Country people tended to share the meat and vegetables from their farms and gardens without a second thought. They had pork chop dinners and fish frys and pancake breakfasts to raise money for special events.

They had church-sponsored picnics to celebrate the beginning and end of school at the community park. They wore hats on Sunday and kept monogrammed handkerchiefs in their coat or pants pockets.

They were generally free talking even when they weren't necessarily open-minded and anybody who had the time to talk always had something to say about the weather: "How many inches of rain did you get at your house?" "How hot is it supposed to get today?" "Ain't that humidity high?" "Feels like tornado weather." "Watch out, it's lightning." "And man, that wind chill is a real mother."

Now people were discussing the murders of Kandi Kane and Stella Fitzgerald. They were wondering if the new fellow in town would be able to help the GPD do their job. After all, what was a detective supposed to do besides detect? This event had catapulted Kenneth away from who-is-that-guy status to THAT GUY status.

It was a way of living that deserved protecting as much as any endangered species out in the wild. In Guthrie, men and women still cooked food from scratch, neighbors watched over children at play, and when someone died, food was carried over to the survivors and hugs were given freely right along with wisdom and the best method for getting things done right.

It was small-town living at its finest and that's why Daisy couldn't hide under the covers no matter how much she wanted to do so: The snake had to be found and cast out of paradise. That Kenneth recognized this, too, was a bonus.

Daisy loved him all the more for his quiet dedication, his steadfast attention to words and deeds she wasn't paying attention to because she saw them everyday.

"I'm thinking of the use of the word *Oakies* as sarcasm," he said. "Sarcasm is sometimes triggered when a person feels threatened. It could have been a way for her to hide her true feelings during a sudden encounter by a flash from the past."

For the first time in a while, Daisy was confused. They'd been on a roll and now her mind was tripped up. "Are you referring to Sugar or Kandi?"

"Both. Don't forget, Sugar was walking in her mother's footsteps. The women did not come to your place together. They met after Kandi left here. Somehow they made it to Wal-Mart where they got into a public scuffle. They didn't stay at the same hotel. Kandi wound up dead and Sugar was running all over the place trying to find out what happened."

Daisy was back on the same page. "Guilty conscience."

"Yes," Kenneth said. "What if Kandi told Sugar who she saw at Wal-Mart and why she was so ticked off? What if Sugar told her mother she was being paranoid and then when her mother wound up dead, she felt so shocked and ashamed of herself, she started searching for the killer herself at the garden show? It would explain why Sugar was so frantic."

Daisy had a problem with that idea. "But if Sugar was at Wal-Mart, she'd know who the killer was."

"Not necessarily. Rita didn't say Kandi blew up at any one person in particular. She blew up in general."

Daisy leaned her head back against the sofa, eyes half-closed, her words directed at the ceiling. "So maybe Sugar was getting in everybody's face to try to see if she could recognize a face from Wal-Mart?"

"That's exactly what I'm thinking," Kenneth said. "This would make sense of Sugar's persistent attitude, considering that her mother had just been murdered. I'd have thought she'd be prone with grief."

Daisy said, "In TV shows, people act that way

all the time. Out of touch with death. Almost normal. I guess that's a kind of shock."

He gave her a you-and-that-stupid-TV look. "This isn't make believe, Daisy. You've got to stay focused here."

She lifted her head to stare at him as if he was the one who wasn't making sense. "I know. I'm just trying to point out that Sugar didn't have all her marbles to start with. Neither did Kandi or Stella. That's a connection."

Kenneth laughed. "You are something else." She matched his thinking and doing with creativity and mandala-style thinking: round and round with circles connecting.

With Daisy, everything touched and moved together, even if it didn't touch or move at the same time. He was as surprised by what happened and affected as deeply as she was, although his emotions were centered around her safety and her emotions were centered around the people she knew and loved, the people she trusted.

In turn, she thought Kenneth was the most dynamic man she'd ever met. He had muscle. He had brains. Right now, he was an anchor. "Thank you for . . . being you."

It was while he was looking into Daisy's eyes that Kenneth realized he'd been working the puzzle the wrong way by focusing his attention on Kandi. Kandi had a lot of enemies, Stella did not. Stella lived in Guthrie. She knew precisely who it was that struck the fatal blow. Daisy's eyes were trusting, possibly as trusting as Stella's eyes were when she faced the last person she would ever see: her killer.

Kenneth said, "When we arrived at Stella's house, she told your mother that 'a real journalist is always open to surprise encounters. They might lead to unique revelations.' "

Daisy gave him a give-me-a-break look. "Speak English."

"That's pretty much what your mother said. She also called Stella a frustrated singer and a fake journalist."

"Not in those words exactly, but that was the general idea," Daisy said. "I remember Stella was mad enough to take a swing at Mom. I think it took all her common sense not to do it."

"Anger," Kenneth said, as if every clue had clicked into place. "Intense, uncontrollable outrage that led to a sudden wild outburst."

"Just like the way Kandi behaved in Wal-Mart."

"Right. Your mother and Stella ran into each other at the beauty salon and that's when Stella hinted she knew something your mother would want to know, too."

"I keep forgetting about that."

"Who owns the salon?"

Daisy's mental wheels were turning at a painful rate. Slowly and very softly, she said, "Zenith."

"So Zenith might know more than she thinks."

"Probably."

"Did she ever talk to you about what happened at the beauty salon that day?"

Daisy was surprised to find herself being interrogated. She'd always imagined bright lights in a cold and sterile room with bare walls and a scratched wood table with even more raggedy wood chairs. "Yes."

"What did she say?"

"Well, we were at the garden show and we saw . . ." Daisy was shaking her head no, her left hand over her mouth, which had fallen open.

Kenneth tensed immediately, but he stayed put. "What is it?"

Daisy jumped to her feet and started pacing. She quit pacing and hurried into the kitchen. In the familiar comfort of her kitchen, she poured herself one more cup of coffee and threw back a swallow that was so hot it burned her throat and added to the tears that had come to her eyes.

"No," she said, "no."

"Daisy?"

Daisy flopped down in one of the kitchen chairs. "Mr. Dillingsworth."

"What about him?"

"He did it."

Maybe, Kenneth thought, they really had fallen into a parallel dimension, a place where nothing familiar made sense anymore. He sat down beside her and wiped her tears away with his thumbs. He kissed her right cheek, her soft brown lips, her trembling and scratched chin. "How do you know?"

"Number one, we've run out of suspects, which is what we were trying to do: eliminate them by examining the evidence we knew as fact. Number two, I remember that Mr. Dillingsworth asked me a lot of questions about Kandi. He wanted to know where she was staying. He's the only person who asked me that. It was like he wanted to confirm it or something. He also asked me where Stella was and . . . and . . . I . . . uh, I can't breathe."

"Take your time."

"I told him she was in the hospitality room."

Kenneth spoke quietly. "He's also a founding member of the garden club and on the event planning committee. I can understand why you wouldn't be suspicious of his questions. Hell, I'm even surprised."

"Well, I was thinking about Stella. The killer had to be someone benign, someone even she trusted. We all trusted Mr. Dillingsworth. All of us. Stella was going to kick Mom's butt just for saying something she didn't like. Mom would never have been able to take Stella by surprise."

Kenneth massaged her hands between his own. Her fingers felt stiff and cold. "You're using your mother as a comparison stick."

"Yes. I couldn't have got that close to Stella because I'm Rita's daughter. Zenith couldn't because she's my best friend and she's crazy about my mom. Neither myself nor Zenith would allow them to fight anyway. Stella would know this and so her trust in us wouldn't be complete."

Kenneth saw the writing on the wall. "Cinnamon couldn't have got that close because Stella didn't trust her to start with. Few people trust a gossip and that's exactly what Cinnamon is—a gossip."

Daisy wiped her face with a napkin and straightened her back, squared her shoulders and lifted her chin. This was no time to fall apart. "Right."

"Go on."

"The only other person with access to all information and places was Mr. Dillingsworth. Even though he's in his early seventies, he's strong. He's always lifting and hauling and moving and he manhandles his big stinking diesel truck like it's a mid-size SUV. It wouldn't take more than one hard swing to kill either Kandi or Stella and he could do that if he wanted to do it. One swing that is."

Daisy knew she wasn't making perfect sense but she was getting her theory out the best way she could. Kenneth was smart enough to figure out what was what. He was smart enough to just listen.

After a moment, he asked the stickiest question of all, the one question Daisy had no idea how to answer: "But why would he do it?"

Daisy was fidgeting. "Maybe that's the secret that Stella found out—a connection between Dillingsworth and Kandi's past. Maybe she didn't even know how important the information she had was until Kandi was killed. When Dillingsworth approached her to confront her about whatever it was she knew, she still trusted him not to kill her. That's why she didn't fight him."

Kenneth extended his arms in front of him. He opened and closed his fists as if to stretch his fingers. He rolled his neck from side to side. He just didn't get it. Dillingsworth was neat, kind, well-spoken, and well liked. "What could make him desperate or angry enough to kill a friend?"

"The same thing that made Kandi flip her lid at Wal-Mart. The past."

Kenneth simply nodded.

Daisy went to sit in his lap. She rested her head on his shoulder. She felt his warmth and his beating heart and knew there was no other place she'd rather be than sitting in the kitchen with his arms around her. She felt safe and sad and ready to put the whole sorry mess behind them both. "Yeah. The past."

"I'll call Spud and have him notify the right people. They'll want to talk to Dillingsworth tonight."

Within hours, Spud called them back to report his findings. He'd learned the sordid and simple truth about Kandi Kane's and Stella Fitzgerald's killer: Mr. Dillingsworth was the murderous friend they'd been searching for. The case was closed.

Mr. Dillingsworth was the father of Bootsie, the woman who Kandi Kane's husband had an affair with, the woman Kandi saw on video, the woman who caused Kandi's divorce and flight from home.

Mr. Dillingsworth's daughter had never left the town where she'd been raised with Kandi. Distraught over her own breakup with Kandi's husband, Bootsie had been drinking away her sorrows and had crashed her small sedan into a tree, less than a year after Kandi's divorce. Bootsie hadn't survived the crash.

Irrationally, Mr. Dillingsworth blamed Kandi. He'd seen Sugar around town and her young face reminded him so much of Kandi in her youth that when he saw Kandi at Wal-Mart, all his old anger returned to the surface. He'd approached Kandi at her hotel. He and Kandi had argued and he'd killed her.

Apparently, Sugar had visited Cinnamon's antique store on Harrison. Somehow they'd rolled around to the subject of Sugar's background. Dillingsworth was at Cinnamon's store to discuss the garden show with her. He made the mistake of telling Sugar he was an old friend of her mother's. Cinnamon, being her usual gossiping self, mentioned this to Stella.

Stella wanted to break into society journalism and thought she might be able to use whatever she found out about Dillingsworth and Kandi as a way to connect the garden show with a highly visible local society person.

Dillingsworth was well-to-do and a generous Guthrie philanthropist. He got wind of Stella's background checking and confronted her in the hospitality room. In a fit of anger, similar to what he felt against Kandi before he killed her, he whacked Stella over the head and killed her, too.

Apparently, he used gardening as a method of anger management. Gardening made him feel peaceful, and his rivalry with Zenith gave him the edge he needed to work off his competitive spirit. His age, his social influence, his amiable nature all contributed to his camouflage. Everybody trusted him. This included Spud Gurber, the garden club, Daisy and . . . even Kenneth Gunn.

Epilogue

It was Sunday afternoon. Daisy's admiration for Kenneth had reached a new height. Never had she imagined they would solve a local mystery together. Not once had he wavered in his desire to protect her from danger. Not once had he let her down.

Quietly and diligently, he had worked behind the scenes, careful not to interfere with the on-going police investigations. While she struggled to hold her special event together, he'd refereed feuding garden club members and grappled with news-hungry rubberneckers. Best of all, he'd carved out time to make her feel cherished as they hunted for means and motive in a drama that brought them closer together than ever before.

As polite as he'd been to her customers, family and friends, Kenneth had treated them all with equal doses of suspicion. Most important to Daisy, he'd been at her side during the crucial moment when she identified the killer.

The future was bright. People were clamoring for another garden show, this time during the spring season. In the end, Daisy's original goal was achieved: to have a well-received flower show and exhibition.

On the last night of Kenneth's vacation, it was Daisy who wanted him to remain, not because he wanted to be there whether she lived in Guthrie or not, but because she was there and because she needed the comfort of his love.

And so it was that in the cool quiet of her bedroom, Daisy used her body, her lips, her soul to express the full weight of her commitment. She worked her special magic until Kenneth cried hoarsely, "Enough!"

Her laugh was delicious, the sound of it low and seductive. She had him right where she wanted him: in her bed and in her arms.

His palms squeezed her thighs. "My offer was accepted on the Midwest Boulevard property."

She licked his ear. "What about your condo?"

"I'll lease it. I've got a friend who's been looking for a place to use as temporary housing for visiting business execs."

"Perfect."

"Yeah."

When Daisy realized he was enjoying their soft afterplay as much as she was, a glow of solace released itself inside her. She slid gracefully over his body, feeling his breath come apart as her heat touched him from his bottom to his top. Sensations shimmied through her body. At random intervals, desire danced over her skin.

He eased the fingertips of both hands over her bare back in soothing moves that teased and pleased her. With a sigh that spoke of sheer rightness, she lay her cheek against his shoulder, pressing a caress to the tender hollow of his throat.

Focused, he welcomed the warm weight of her body. With each breath, their chests rose and fell together. Heat melded and grew hot, then hotter as their legs intertwined and their hearts quickened in beat. There was no rush, not anymore and not ever again. They had all the time in the world from now on, and the world belonged to them.

Kenneth closed his eyes and listened to what her spirit was telling him. Everything it said, everywhere it touched, was exquisite. She was exquisite. He brought his hand to her face, traced her cheek, her chin, her lips, the lashes that brought shade and shelter to her beautiful brown eyes. Home. Daisy was home.

At last, and after a very long while, it was she who broke their intimate spell, she who allowed the low-burning flame between them to lick her from the inside out and from the top to the bottom. Her palm caressed him here . . . there . . . everywhere.

The kiss between them began soft and ended sexy. Nothing separated them, nothing at all. When kissing and holding and hugging was no longer enough, Kenneth joined them as one so that together they celebrated the different tastes and textures that made them uniquely male and female.

In response, she flung her head back, the move exposing her to his view completely, only for Kenneth. Always . . . for Kenneth. He was her earth and her sun. Nothing mattered beyond his touch—sometimes rough, sometimes gentle, always right.

And then finally, they soared together, each blinded to light, each oblivious to sound, both profoundly moved by the beauty and the strength of their love, a love that was more than simply wonderful, it was simply marvelous.

Dear Reader:

As always, I hope you enjoyed this latest story. While some landmarks and businesses are true to Guthrie, SIMPLY MARVELOUS is a work of fiction.

When you have the time, I hope you will share your opinions with me. If you do, please be sure to include a self-addressed, stamped envelope with your letter. I can be reached at: P.O. Box 253, Guthrie, OK 73044.

Sincerely,
Shelby Lewis